W9-DFG-820

Valene can't believe Jordan enjoys spending time with her.

"I guess I'd better be going," Jordan said. "I've got another early morning meeting scheduled with my work crew, but I'll be home about four. I could drive you to see Hero again. Maybe Jeff'll want to come along this time."

"I'd like that," Valene said. "Are you sure it won't inconvenience you?"

"Not at all. I want to drive you. I like being with you."

She felt herself blushing. She liked being with him too, but she'd never tell him.

He leaned down and planted a quick kiss on her cheek. "See you about four tomorrow."

His sudden kiss rendered her speechless. "I. . .ah. . .yes, four. See you then."

She watched as he strode down her sidewalk and turned toward his condo. *Oh, dear Lord. I think I'm falling in love. Jordan is everything I could ever want in a man. But why would he ever want me?*

JOYCE LIVINGSTON has done many things in her life (in addition to being a wife, mother of six, and grandmother to oodles of grandkids, all of whom she loves dearly). From being a television broadcaster for eighteen years, to lecturing and teaching on quilting and sewing, to writing magazine articles on a variety of subjects. She's danced with Lawrence Welk, ice-skated with a Chimpanzee, had bottles broken over her head by stuntmen, interviewed hundreds of celebrities and controversial figures, and many other interesting and unusual things. But now, when she isn't off traveling to wonderful and exotic places as a part-time tour escort, her days are spent sitting in front of her computer, creating stories. She feels her writing is a ministry and a calling from God, and she hopes Heartsong readers will be touched and uplifted by what she writes. Joyce loves to hear from her readers and invites you to visit her on the Internet at: www.joycelivingston.com

Books by Joyce Livingston

HEARTSONG PRESENTS
HP353—Ice Castle
HP382—The Bride Wore Boots
HP437—Northern Exposure
HP516—Lucy's Quilt
HP521—Be My Valentine

Love Is Kind

Joyce Livingston

Heartsong Presents

I would like to dedicate this book to my irreplaceable black Lab and best friend, Lancelot. We lost Lancelot three years ago after having had him with us for seventeen years. Although he was an outdoor dog, he and I spent many happy hours together, swimming in the lake, planting flowers, chasing one another, and just sitting enjoying each other's company. I love you, Lancelot, and miss you terribly. You were a good doggie.

A note from the Author:
I love to hear from my readers! You may correspond with me by writing:

Joyce Livingston
Author Relations
PO Box 719
Uhrichsville, OH 44683

ISBN 1-58660-807-X

LOVE IS KIND

All Scripture quotations are taken from the King James Version of the Bible.

PRINTED IN THE U.S.A.

one

Valene Zobel blinked back tears as she slipped the smoky blue, satin dress onto a padded hanger and placed it in her closet. How she was going to miss her twin.

"Why're you crying, Aunt Val? Weddings are supposed to make you happy. That's what my daddy said."

She pulled her new nephew close and ran her fingers through his hair. "I am happy, Jeff. Sometimes grownups cry when they're happy. It's just that I'm going to miss Vanessa. Now that she and your daddy are married, we won't be together as much."

The boy seemed satisfied with her answer and turned his attention toward Hero, the big black Labrador Vanessa had given Valene several months ago. "Come on, Boy. Wanna watch me ride my new bike?"

Hero seemed happy with the idea, and the two of them raced off to retrieve the little bike from the living room of Valene's first-floor condo.

"Jeff!" she called out after him, remembering the rules Nathan had laid down before he and her sister had taken off on their honeymoon to Ireland. "You can only ride your bike on the sidewalk! Not on the parking lot! And wear your helmet! Do you hear me?"

Jeff nodded over his shoulder as he mounted his prized possession, the shiny red bicycle his new step-mom had given him.

Valene had looked forward to being Jeff's baby-sitter while they were gone. She grinned as he slipped the helmet on his head and took off down the sidewalk, with Hero nipping at his heels. What was it her twin sister had told her when she'd given her that cute little six-month-old puppy to bribe her to do her taxes for her? Flattering her by telling her that she was the smart one? The valedictorian who could do anything with numbers?

I might be good with numbers, but I must be lacking in other areas of my life, or today's wedding could've been a double wedding. I didn't even catch the bridal bouquet!

"Be careful, Jeff!" she yelled out loudly, cupping her hands to her mouth. "I don't want you getting any skinned knees while your dad is away!"

She stood in the open doorway, watching, wondering what it would be like to find that perfect man, like Vanessa had when Nathan appeared in her life. She smiled as she recalled the funny way he and her sister had met, laughing aloud as she remembered the expression on Nathan's face when he'd first seen the two of them together. He'd done a double take, then blurted out, "You're twins!"

Valene had wanted to say, "Duh! You're kidding!" but had refrained. Words like those might've come from Vanessa's mouth, but not hers. She'd never say anything that might offend or embarrass someone. How was she ever going to get along without her twin now that Vanessa was married? Just thinking about it made her sad.

"Watch, Aunt Valene! Watch me! I can ride really fast!"

"Remember what I said about—" Realizing what was about to happen, she screamed out, "Jeff! Watch out!" She ran toward him, picking up her pace with each stride, frantically waving her arms, trying to get his attention.

It was too late.

Instead of stopping where the sidewalk ended, the bicycle whizzed onto the crowded parking lot at full speed, right into the path of an approaching pickup truck.

A small boy's scream, the screeching of brakes, and the sound of a sudden thud, all seemed to happen in slow motion as Valene raced into the lot, weaving her way among the parked cars, her heart pounding furiously, her mind whirring with thoughts of what if?

"I didn't see him coming! Honest I didn't!" the driver yelled out as he leaped from the oversized pickup and raced around to the front. "I tried to stop—"

"Jeff!"

"I'm sorry, Aunt Valene."

She blinked hard, breathing a prayer of thanks, her palm flattening against her chest as she heard the boy's petulant voice. There was Jeff, on the other side of the truck, still straddling his bike. He was okay.

But the man was bending over someone.

Who?

After wrapping her arms about Jeff and making sure he hadn't sustained any injuries, Val cautioned him to stay put before hurrying to see if she should call for an ambulance.

But the man wasn't leaning over a person.

He was leaning over Hero, and the big dog wasn't moving. He was lying frighteningly still in a small pool of blood.

"I didn't mean to hit him! I didn't see him! Oh, why did this have to happen? I never meant to do it! I hit the brakes when I saw the boy, but—"

Weeping, Valene dropped onto her knees and tried to comfort Hero, stroking his head frantically.

"We need to get him to a vet!" the man said, stooping beside her and carefully scooping up the dog in his long arms, his face filled with sheer panic. "I can't leave him here to die. He needs attention immediately!"

"But—"

"Hurry!" the man ordered, moving quickly to his spotlessly clean truck and carefully lowering the injured dog onto the leather backseat. "Let's hope we're not too late."

"But, Jeff—" Valene said, almost incoherently. "What—"

"Hurry," the man said again.

Almost robotically, she rushed back to her apartment and grabbed her purse before closing and locking the door.

"You ride in the backseat with your dog. Your son can ride up front with me. Now hurry!" the man told her in a take-charge manner, although he seemed to be shaking as badly as she was.

He placed the shiny red bike in the truck's bed while Valene and Jeff crawled inside. "You'll have to help me. Where's the closest vet or animal hospital?"

"Ah, let me think. Dr. Bainbridge's clinic is. . .is. . ." For a moment, Val's mind went blank. "Two blocks down and. . . and turn to the left—no right."

The man's concerned gaze caught hers in the rearview mirror, and she could see tears in his eyes. "Which is it? Left or right?"

"Right. It's right. About three blocks." *I've got to settle down,* she told herself, taking a deep breath before continuing. "It. . .It's across from the shopping center. A red brick building, I think. It's an animal hospital and clinic. I–I took Hero there for his shots."

For the first time, she became fully aware of the turmoil the man must be experiencing. He'd nearly hit a boy on a bicycle. He could've killed Jeff. She couldn't even begin to imagine how she would feel if the same thing had happened to her, and suddenly, instead of anger, she felt sorry for him. All this time she'd been so concerned about Jeff, then Hero, she hadn't even considered how he must be feeling. "Ar–are you alright?" she mumbled through chattering teeth. "I mean, you. . ."

He nodded but kept watch on the road. "I–I'll be okay. Just a little shook up. Don't worry about me. You take care of that dog. He's the important one here. I'll have us there in a flash. What's your name?"

"I'm Valene Zobel. Jeff is my nephew, not my son. He's staying with me this week." A shudder passed through her body as she slipped her free hand over the seat and squeezed Jeff's slim shoulders. How close she'd come to losing him. *Thank You, Lord. If that truck had been just one second—*

"My mom got really sick and died a long time ago," Jeff said sadly. "Vanessa is my new mama. She's nice."

"I'm Jordan Young." The driver gave them a quick sideways glance, then turned his attention back to the oncoming traffic.

Within minutes, the truck pulled into the vet's parking lot. The driver leaped out, jerked open the back door, scooped Hero up, and dashed toward the clinic. Valene grabbed Jeff's hand, and the two ran in behind the man named Jordan.

The receptionist took one look at Hero and quickly called out for the doctor on duty as she guided the truck's driver toward an examination room.

"I'll need some information," she told him, motioning toward a desk in the lobby. "Your wife can stay here with the dog while we fill out a few papers."

Clutching Jeff's hand tightly, her fingers entwined with his, Valene inserted, "I'm not—"

But the man who'd introduced himself as Jordan Young took hold of her arm and stopped her. "It's okay. Stay with your dog." For the first time since the accident, his chiseled features softened a bit and he smiled. "Hero. Isn't that what you called him?"

She nodded, finding it hard to speak without crying.

"I'll take care of everything. After all, I'm the one who. . ." He paused, and she could see his Adam's apple rise and fall as he swallowed hard. "Who caused his injuries."

"But you didn't. I—"

He wagged a cautioning finger to silence her. "We'll worry about where the blame goes later. Right now, you need to be with Hero."

After spending several minutes checking Hero, Dr. Bainbridge momentarily diverted his attention from the limp, banged up body on the table to Valene. "This dog's injuries seem pretty serious. It might help if you'd talk to him a bit. He might not hear you, but then again, he might. Right now, I think he could use a few words of encouragement."

Valene gathered her shoulder-length hair in one hand and pulled it to the side as she leaned over Hero and whispered into his ear. "I love you, Hero." She gulped hard, barely able to continue as the tears rolled down her cheeks. "I need you, Hero. Please don't die. Please—"

She felt a slight tug on her sleeve, and pulling herself away from her beloved Hero, she looked into the worried, tear-stained face of the six year old. "Is he gonna die?"

"Oh, no, Sweetie." Valene gulped hard and forced a smile as she pulled her nephew close and held him tight. "I'm sure the doctor is going to fix him up just fine."

"You'd better go now," the veterinarian told them as he pulled a curtain about the tiny examination area. "We're going to do the best we can for Hero. You can wait in the lobby if you want, but it may be awhile before we can tell you anything for certain, after I've done a more thorough examination and we've X-rayed him. If his injuries are as extensive as I fear they might be, he's going to require some long-term care."

"But you will be able to save him, won't you, Doc?" a trembling male voice asked.

Valene turned and found the man whose truck had hit Hero standing beside her, apparently finished filling out the necessary papers.

Jordan Young's hand cupped the doctor's shoulder. "You gotta save him, Doc. He can't die!"

The doctor stood upright and hung his stethoscope about his thick neck. "What happens to Hero from here on out somewhat depends on you folks."

Valene's gaze went to the doctor as she found herself finally able to speak. "What do you mean, depends on us?" She dabbed at her eyes, feeling slightly offended by his words. "Of course, I want him to be alright. He's my dog and I love him. I'll do anything to keep him alive."

Jordan pulled a handkerchief from his back pocket and wiped at the beads of perspiration forming on his forehead. "Me too, Doc. That dog has got to live."

"Does that mean he's gonna die, Aunt Val?" Jeff asked with big eyes as he stared at the still figure on the table.

Before she could answer, with a reassuring smile, Jordan slipped an arm about Jeff's shoulders. "Hey, don't you worry. I'll betcha the doc'll be able to fix him up just fine."

The doctor seemed to be assessing their words carefully before speaking. "I have to be brutally frank with you. The possible surgery and long-term care we're talking about can get pretty expensive. Many folks decide to put their animals to sleep rather than go to such an expense."

Valene gasped. "Put Hero to sleep? I'd never do that!"

"Do whatever is necessary to get that dog well, Doc. I'm footing the bill on this. I don't care what it costs. I'm the one who hit him, and I aim to do the right thing."

With a raise of his brows, the veterinarian shrugged.

"Well, like I said, the decision is up to you and your wife. I'll do whatever you tell me. I never like putting a dog down, especially when I can see how much he's loved."

Valene clung tightly to Jeff's hand. She started to speak, to correct the doctor's misapprehension but felt a reassuring arm slip about her shoulders. A feeling of gratitude warmed her heart and kept her silent. They could straighten the doctor out later. Hero's welfare was the important thing right now.

"Do it, Doc." Jordan Young's tone was firm and unwavering. "I've already given my credit card to your receptionist. It's as good as paid for."

Dr. Bainbridge looked from one to the other. "Just wanted to make sure you and your wife know what you're getting into. Like I said, some folks—"

"I don't care what some other folks do, Doc," Jordan Young answered quickly, breaking into the man's sentence. "Do everything you can for Hero. No matter what it costs."

Valene was so relieved she wanted to throw her arms about Jordan's neck. Although her thoughts had been focused on Hero and his injuries, she had to admit she had been concerned about the cost. Not that she'd ever let the doctor put Hero down, as he'd so delicately put it. She wouldn't. She'd find the money somewhere, even if she had to refinance her nearly paid-off car. But his words had set her mind at ease.

"Hero? That's his name?" the kindly doctor asked with a slight grin as he placed a gentle hand on the big dog's back.

Valene nodded, still blinking back tears.

"He's Lick's brother," Jeff inserted, his eyes rounded with fear. "Lick's real name is Licorice."

"Hero and Lick came from the same litter. Lick is Jeff's dog," Valene explained in a shaky voice.

The doctor bent and clamped a firm, reassuring hand on Jeff's shoulder. "Well, don't you worry, young man. We're going to take good care of Hero." He motioned Valene and Jordan toward the door. "You two take your son and go on into the waiting room. Once I've taken some X-rays, I'll be able to tell you more about his injuries."

"But. . ." Valene sent a quick glance at the man standing beside her.

"I think we'd better do as the doc says." Jordan gestured toward the door.

She paused a second then, realizing how unimportant it was that the doctor know they weren't husband and wife, moved toward him, tugging on Jeff's hand.

"I'll come out for you as soon as I've finished," the doctor called out just before he closed the door behind him.

The three seated themselves in a corner, with Valene and Jeff on one side of a little square table, and Jordan on the other. She slipped an arm about Jeff, then bowed her head and prayed silently, asking God to be with Hero. When she opened her eyes, she found Jordan Young staring at her.

"I'm—I'm sorry about hitting your dog. If only I'd—"

"It wasn't your fault," Valene said, turning to face him. His cheeks were flushed, and although it was cool in the room, he was still perspiring.

"It was my fault," Jeff said, his rounded eyes filling with tears. "Aunt Val told me to stay on the sidewalk, and I didn't do it."

"I guess we were all at fault," Valene said in a raspy voice as she wrapped an arm about her nephew and drew him close. "Letting you ride your bicycle on that narrow sidewalk wasn't the smartest thing I've ever done. I knew it dead-ended at the parking lot. I just didn't think to tell you."

Jordan pulled out his handkerchief and dabbed at his forehead again. "I'm sorry I hit Hero, but I'm glad it wasn't the boy. I could never have lived with myself if—"

"But you didn't hit him," she reminded Jordan, trying to control her voice and the turmoil still going on inside her. "Neither Jeff nor Hero should have been in that parking lot."

She stared at him, trying to comprehend the pain and fear he must've felt when he thought he'd hit Jeff. No wonder the man was shook up. How would she feel if the same thing had happened to her? "Normally, I never let Hero outside unless I have him on a leash." She watched as a slight smile curled at the corners of his strong mouth.

"I know. I've seen you walking him." His grin turned into a full smile. "Or should I say, him walking you?"

She smiled back. "He does tend to get a bit rambunctious sometimes."

Jeff frowned and yanked on her sleeve. "What's a ram-but-yus, Aunt Val?"

She placed a loving hand on his shoulder and gave it a gentle pat. "It means, sometimes he wants to run and check everything out when I want him to walk."

Jeff nodded and seemed satisfied with her answer.

"Hero, huh? That's quite a name for a dog." Jordan's eyes twinkled, and he seemed to be a bit more relaxed than when they'd first sat down. "How'd you come up with it?"

Valene let out a slight chuckle. "You'll probably laugh at me."

He grinned. "I'll try not to."

"My twin sister, Vanessa, gave him to me when I moved into my condo. We both love animals. In fact, she owns a pet store. Whiskers, Wags, and Wings. She thought I needed a dog for protection. This is the first time I've ever lived alone."

"Vanessa is my new mother," Jeff inserted.

"Vanessa and Jeff's dad were married today."

Jordan's jaw dropped. "Today?"

"I was the ring bear!" Jeff lifted his head proudly.

Valene smiled back when Jordan sent her an amused grin.

"Ring bear-er," she corrected, running her hand across her new nephew's back.

"Ring bear-er," he repeated.

She pulled a children's magazine from the stack on the table and handed it to Jeff. He opened it and immediately began perusing the words.

"Anyway," Valene went on, "since my new dog was supposed to be my protector, I named him Hero. Kinda dumb, huh?"

"No, not dumb at all. I like the name. It suits him."

"He's a good dog, and I feel much safer having him around. Especially at night."

"A woman can't be too careful."

They sat in an awkward silence for a few minutes, the ticking of the clock on the wall and the sound of Jeff turning the pages the only sounds in the room. For the first time since entering the clinic, Valene became aware of the faint, clean smell of antiseptic. She glanced across the room at a man sitting opposite them, grimly holding onto a small cat who seemed frightfully thin. She couldn't help but wonder why the man had brought the cat in. Maybe it was there to be spayed.

"Doesn't Jeff go to school?" Jordan asked, his gaze going to the boy.

Her attention was quickly drawn away from the cat. "Yes, but they're having a state teachers' meeting next Thursday and Friday. School will be out anyway, so my new brother-in-law figured it wouldn't hurt Jeff to miss a couple of days and come to Spring Valley and spend the week with me. He's a bright kid and can make up the missed work easily."

The receptionist appeared. "Mr. and Mrs. Young, Dr. Bainbridge is ready to see you now."

The three filed quickly back into the little room where Hero still lay on the table.

"How is he, Doc?" Jordan asked, stepping quickly to the dog's side.

two

Dr. Bainbridge pulled off his glasses and rubbed at his eyes. "Well, I'm afraid I have some bad news."

Valene let out a gasp as she stared at the still figure on the table. "Is he—"

"No, he's alive," Dr. Bainbridge assured her quickly. "I've given him something to make him rest."

"You can't let him die," Jordan said quickly, leaning over the still body on the table. "Please, Doc. Please!"

The doctor held up a palm toward them. "He's not going to die, but he is going to require a lot of care. Maybe more than you two are willing to give him."

"What's wrong with him?" Jordan asked, wringing his hands, his face void of color.

Valene found herself full of questions but knew if she tried to verbalize one word she'd begin to cry. *Hero! Oh, Hero! Why did I ever let you out without your leash?*

"Other than the obvious skin abrasions your dog has sustained, I'd thought perhaps his leg was broken." The man paused. "A broken leg would have been simple. I could've put a pin in it, and in a few days he'd be running around, almost as if the accident had never happened. But. . ."

"But what?" Jordan and Valene asked in unison.

"I'm sorry to say, his injuries weren't that simple. I hate to have to tell you this. He has a fractured pelvis."

Valene's tears gushed forth unashamedly. During her time at the pet store, she'd heard horror stories about dogs who'd fractured their pelvis and how long it had taken them to recover. Not Hero! Not her precious Hero!

Jordan raked his hands through his hair. "Exactly what does that mean? Surgery? Will he recover?"

"Oh, yes. He'll recover, in time. As to surgery? There's really nothing I can do. Dogs are different than people. That pelvis will heal by itself. Eventually. But in the meantime, you'll have to do everything for him." He paused as a deep frown creased his forehead. "And I mean everything. Twenty-four/seven. He'll be helpless and totally dependent on you."

"For how long?" Valene asked, finally able to string three words together without crying.

"A good six to eight weeks."

"Then?"

"Then, other than quite a bit of stiffness in his hind end, he should be fine. God, in His infinite wisdom, made us so these old bodies will heal. Dogs too." The doctor gestured toward Hero. "I know he looks pretty sad right now with all those abrasions, but they'll heal and his fur will grow back. It's the inside I'm concerned about. I'd like to keep him here for a few days, then you can take him home."

Valene prayed in her heart, thanking God. Hero was going to live, and in time, he'd be his old self.

"That is, if you're sure you want to take on the responsibility of caring for him," the doctor cautioned. "It's not going to be easy. He won't be able to use his back legs at all for awhile."

She drew in a sharp breath and held it.

"He'll try to get up and walk. It's a dog's nature to want to move around, even when he's in pain. He'll try to drag himself by using his front legs, and there won't be much you can do to stop him. Because of those natural tendencies, you may want limit his space by keeping him in a box of some sort, when you're not helping him exercise. And let me tell you, it's gonna get messy! He's gonna be worse than a newborn baby. Only he won't be wearing diapers, if you get what I mean."

Valene nodded as she tried to imagine managing a nearly sixty-pound dog and his bodily functions.

"What about pain, Doc?" Jordan asked, seeming to grasp the doctor's implications as to the problems Hero's injuries would cause. "He's got to be in terrible pain."

The doctor nodded. "You're right. His pain is probably almost unbearable. I'll be giving him about one hundred milligrams of Rimadyl twice a day. That should keep him fairly comfortable. And for those abrasions, he'll be getting an amoxicillin tablet twice a day to make sure no infection sets in and that those injuries heal up properly."

"Will we need to keep some kind of salve on them?" Valene asked, trying to take in everything the doctor was saying.

"No. No salve. Wouldn't stay on. He'd lick it off. The tablets work much better, but the wounds will have to be kept clean at all times." He crossed his arms and leaned against the table, his eyes scrutinizing both Valene and Jordan. "Are you sure you want to go through with this? It's not the expense I'm thinking about; it's the inconvenience and time. I want you two to know up front what you're getting into. Taking care of a big dog like this when he's helpless is not going to be an easy task."

He paused, as if giving them time to comment. When neither did, he continued. "It's not too late to change your minds. If you're not up to doing this, it'd be better for Hero if you put him down now. He can't make it without you. It's going to be hard on him too."

Valene's jaw dropped. "I don't care how much care he takes. I'll do it gladly!"

Jordan stepped up beside her, and she felt his arm slide about her shoulders. "I live nearby. I'm going to help her."

Dr. Bainbridge adjusted his glasses and gave them a funny stare. "You—you two are separated?"

"No," Jordan inserted awkwardly. "We're neighbors."

Dr. Bainbridge reared back with a laugh. "Oh, excuse me! I thought you two were married! I'm sorry. Oh, my. You were both so concerned, I assumed. . . ." He tugged at his lab coat with a grin. "Guess it's never safe to assume, eh?"

"I should've told you up front," Jordan said, sticking out his hand, "but all I could think about was Hero. I'm Jordan Young."

"I'm Valene Zobel, and this is my nephew, Jeff."

"So, Ms. Zobel, Hero is your dog?"

She nodded. "Yes."

The doctor turned to Jordan. "You were driving the pickup that hit the dog?"

"I'm afraid so."

"Well," Dr. Bainbridge said slowly, rubbing at his forehead, "that does indeed present a problem. I had thought, with you two being married, you could perhaps split the time that's going to be necessary to take care of this dog properly, but with only one person living with—"

"I can take care of him on weekends and some evenings," Jordan volunteered, "and I'll hire someone to help Valene during the week."

The doctor smiled at both of them. "I have a feeling Hero is going to get all the attention he needs. Now," he said, ushering them toward the door, "why don't you all go home and let me tend to your dog?"

Valene stepped aside. "Can I tell him good-bye first?"

When the doctor nodded, she slipped back into the room and bent over the sleeping dog. "I love you, Hero," she whispered. "Don't worry. We're going to do everything we can to get you back on your feet. Just rest, okay?" She stroked his thick, black fur lovingly. "I'll be praying for you."

She looked up to see Jordan standing beside her, his face showing deep concern. He could've yelled at her for letting her dog run loose. There were signs posted all over the condo complex, saying dogs must be kept on a leash at all times. But he hadn't yelled at her. He'd taken the entire blame and not once had he even hinted that she should bear any part of it. Not many men would've been so understanding, and he'd taken on the responsibility of paying all of Hero's bills. "I—I don't know how to thank you," she said, getting bleary-eyed again. "You've been so kind and—"

"Thank me? I hit your dog! I'm surprised you don't hate me!"

"It was my fault. I let him out without his leash."

"That doesn't excuse me. I should've been more observant. What if I'd hit Jeff? I could have, you know."

"I'm so thankful you didn't. I wasn't thinking when I let him ride his bike on that sidewalk."

Jordan shoved his hands into his pants' pockets, rattling his change. "Why don't we quit playing the blame game? It's getting late, and I don't know about you, but I'm hungry. According to the doctor, there's nothing more we can do here."

She glanced at her watch and was surprised to find it was already eight o'clock. "Oh, it is late. Thank you for bringing us, but I have my cell phone. I'll call a cab." She reached out her right hand. "Thank you, Mr. Young. You've been very kind, and I appreciate it."

He ignored her hand and shook his head. "You're not going to call a cab. I brought you, and I'll take you home."

She pulled her phone from her purse. "No, I'll call a cab. You've done quite enough for us."

"Put that thing away. I'm taking you home."

Although tempted, she knew she shouldn't accept his offer. He was nearly a stranger. From childhood, she'd been cautioned to never accept rides from strangers.

"You'll be safe with me," he said with a teasing smile that set her somewhat at ease. "You rode here with me."

She had, and she hadn't even thought to refuse his offer when he'd grabbed up Hero and told her to get into the backseat with the dog. This situation was different, though. Yet wouldn't he think her foolish if she refused, after all they'd shared together? They were going to the same destination. Surely, he wouldn't try anything weird with Jeff around.

"Well, are you coming?"

She hesitated while sending up a quick prayer for discernment. "I–I guess."

He led the way, and soon they were back in his pickup, headed for their condos.

"I'm starving, and I bet you are too," Jordan said as he flipped on the left turn signal and entered the busy street, easily maneuvering into the oncoming traffic. "How about stopping for a burger and fries at Wilbur's Diner? My treat!"

"Oh, no. Thank you anyway. But we couldn't."

He turned his attention away from the street long enough to give her a questioning glance. "Why? You gotta eat too."

"I have things at home to fix. We'll eat there."

"I'll bet Jeff would rather have a burger and fries. Right, Sport?" he asked the boy, catching his attention in the rearview mirror. "Loaded with catsup!"

"Could we, Aunt Val?" Jeff asked, obviously pleased by the man's invitation. "I love fries and catsup."

"No, Jeff. Mr. Young has done quite enough for us. We'll eat at home."

"But, Aunt Val, I—"

"Enough, Jeff," she warned with a frown over her shoulder,

wishing the boy would just settle down and be quiet.

They rode to the condo in silence. As soon as the pickup came to a stop, Jordan rushed around to Valene's door, but she already had it opened and was halfway out. He gave her a quick smile and moved to the back, lowered the tailgate, and pulled out the shiny red bike. "Offer still stands."

She took the bike from his hands and motioned to Jeff to push it toward her condo, then turned back to Jordan. "Thank you. You've been more than kind. But no."

"I'm going to the clinic to see Hero in the morning. I want to make sure he's doing alright. Want to come with me?"

She shook her head. "No, thank you. I don't want to impose."

"Impose? I'd consider it an honor. Not often I get a chance to take a. . ." He paused. Then with a smile that brought out his dimples, he added, "A nice young boy to see a dog."

She couldn't help but laugh. "Really, Mr. Young, we—"

"Jordan," he insisted. "Mr. Young is my father," he added with a snicker.

"Jordan." She liked the sound of his name, and it suited him. It was strong, yet friendly. Not pretentious, but authoritative. "I have a few errands to run tomorrow, so I need to take my car, but thank you for the invitation."

He gave her a shrug. "Well, I'm in 10A. If you change your mind, send Jeff over to tell me, or meet me in the parking lot about eight."

"Thank you, but as I said, I'll be driving. Good night."

He didn't answer but began walking alongside her toward her condo.

"Didn't you say you lived in 10A?"

He nodded. "Yep."

"Isn't it over that way?" she asked, pointing to the next section.

He grinned. "Yep. I'm walking you to your door."

"It really isn't necessary. I think I can make it on my own." She hoped her words didn't sound rude. She didn't mean to be rude; she just didn't know what else to say. Her dealings with handsome men had been quite limited.

"I know. I'm sure you're quite capable. But gentlemen always walk ladies to their door, and. . ." He gave her the grin that brought out his dimples again. "And I like to think of myself as a gentleman."

"Oh," was all Valene could think to say. When they reached her door, she fished her key from her purse and reached toward the keyhole. She wasn't used to having someone watch her do such a mundane task, and his presence unnerved her. What if—when she opened the door—he pushed her inside? He looked like a nice enough guy, but what did she really know about him?

"Are you having trouble with the lock?" he asked, as he leaned in for a better look.

"Aunt Val, open the door!" Jeff said impatiently, his bike leaning against him as he held onto the handlebars.

"Okay." She turned the key and pushed the door open, stood back, and motioned Jeff and the bike inside.

"Good night, Ms. Zobel," Jordan said as he backed away from the door. "I'm sorry about Hero."

"I know you are, and I appreciate your concern. Good night." She closed the door and quickly secured the latch.

"Boy, Aunt Val, that was dumb," Jeff said, as he leaned his bike against the wall. "Now you gotta fix supper."

❧

Jordan sat in the booth at Wilbur's Diner and locked his hands together on the worn Formica-covered tabletop. He'd said he was hungry, but now as he sat in the booth, watching others around him enjoy their food, he wasn't at all sure he wanted to eat. He'd hit a dog. Someone's family pet. He could just as easily have hit a six-year-old boy. A sudden shudder gave him a chill. Things happened so quickly in life. Things for which you couldn't prepare yourself. He well knew.

"What can I get you, Sweetie?"

He pulled his thoughts together and glanced up at the waitress. Although she'd served him dozens of times, he couldn't for the life of him remember her name. "Oh-ah-sorry. I guess my mind was wandering."

"The special is chicken-fried steak with steamed veggies," she told him matter-of-factly. "It's pretty good."

He shook his head. Even the burger and fries, normally his favorite, didn't sound good tonight, not after what he'd been through. "Just a bowl of vegetable soup and a good strong cup of black coffee, please."

"Sure you don't want the steak and veggies, Honey?"

He pushed the menu toward her with another shake of his head. Once he was alone again, he replayed the accident in his mind, wondering if he'd been careless. Had his mind been on something else? He barely remembered seeing Jeff cut out in front of him, and he'd never seen Hero.

"Here's your coffee, Sweetie. Black as night, and strong enough to waddle across the table by itself."

He gave her a feeble smile. "Thanks."

"You feelin' okay? You look a bit pale."

While he appreciated her concern, he didn't feel like explaining. "Long day, that's all."

"You ought to try standing on your feet for ten hours, serving cranky people, then going home to a house full of screaming kids and a useless hubby. Now that's a long day."

He watched as the woman moved to the booth next to him, and for the first time, he noted her slight limp. Funny how you never think about the people around you and what troubles they may be going through. He'd never had a hard day in his life. Not really. Basically he'd had everything he'd ever needed, or wanted, handed to him. Not everyone was that fortunate. He gazed at the busy woman with a new appreciation, deciding to leave her a bigger tip than usual.

The soup arrived, and he spooned up each bite without really tasting it. His mind was still focused on Hero, the little boy, and the woman who'd entered his life so quickly and completely unannounced. What was her story? She'd mentioned she lived alone. Had she been married? A divorcée like a number of the women he'd met since he'd moved into the complex? Was there a significant other in her life? Was that the reason she'd turned down his offer of supper and had nearly turned down a ride home?

He thought about her big, round, blue eyes, eyes that seemed to widen with innocence as she talked. He hadn't noticed those beautiful eyes until they'd reached her condo. Before that, his mind had been centered on the accident.

"More coffee?"

"Ah, no."

"Finished with your soup?"

"Yes. I'd like my bill, please."

"How about a piece of fresh strawberry pie?"

He gave the woman a smile. "No, thanks. Maybe next time."

When she brought the bill, he glanced at it, noted the total, which came to four dollars and thirty-seven cents, pulled out a twenty-dollar bill, and placed it on top.

"Keep the change," he said with a wink as he scooted out of the little booth.

"But this is a twenty!" she said, her voice filled with surprise.

He gave her a grin. "I know."

Valene lay on her back and stared at the ceiling. How could a day that started out so right, end up so wrong? Vanessa's wedding day. The day she and her twin sister had looked forward to since they were old enough to play dress-up. She smiled into the darkness as she remembered the many times they'd played Wedding and how they'd conned their neighbor boy into playing the part of the groom. Their mother had given them an old, white satin party dress that'd yellowed with age, a long piece of white nylon netting to cover their heads as a veil, and a handful of faded silk flowers to use as a bridal bouquet. Whichever girl wasn't being the bride on a given day took the role of the preacher.

What fun they'd had, and what hilarious vows they'd thought up. *Do you take this man to be your husband? Will you keep his clothes washed and ironed, the kitchen clean, and give him pills when he is sick?* They couldn't have been more than five or six at the time, and their groom was at least two years younger and had no idea what he was doing. They just draped him in one of their father's old black jackets and made him stand in front of the make-believe altar—a cardboard box covered with a bath towel.

She and Vanessa would fashion a cross from two small branches they'd break off from the mulberry tree in their backyard. Then they'd stick it into a glob of putty to make it stand. Next to it, they'd place a Bible opened to John 3:16, the first verse they'd ever learned. Since the home-made wedding rings they'd fashion from yellow chenille pipe cleaners were usually misplaced between the mock weddings, their mother had suggested they use the tabs from soda cans, which were a little lopsided in shape but always readily available.

Valene flipped onto her side and scrunched up the pillow beneath her head. Now Vanessa was married. Her twin, her buddy. She couldn't imagine what life was going to be like without her. A ray of moonlight wiggled its way past the edge of the drawn shade and fell across her pillow. She traced its path with her fingertip, wondering where her sister was at that very moment. *Will I ever find that perfect man? The one God has prepared for me?* She frowned as another thought pushed its way into her mind. *What if I never find him? What if God has designed that I remain single?*

A bright light flashed across her room as a car pulled into the parking lot, causing her to blink. *Surely not! Not when He knows all I've ever wanted to be is a wife and a mother.* She thought about Jeff, who was sleeping soundly on her sofa, and how precious he was to Nathan and Vanessa. *Oh, God. Thank You for protecting him.*

Her thoughts went to the man they'd met that day. Was he too lying in bed, trying to sleep? She trembled as she tried to imagine how she would've felt if she'd nearly hit a boy on a bicycle, then hit someone's dog, causing serious injuries. Only now that it was over could she recall the look of panic and guilt she'd seen on Jordan Young's face when she'd rushed into that parking lot. The poor man! Her heart went out to him.

Eventually, sleep overtook her.

❧

Valene jumped when the phone rang at seven. It was Diane, her next-door neighbor. She'd heard about the parking lot accident from another neighbor who'd witnessed it.

"Yes, it was a pretty close call," Valene told her as she filled her in on the details. "But praise God, the truck didn't hit Jeff. Never even grazed him."

"How's Hero?"

Valene swallowed hard. "Not so good." She went on to

explain Hero's injuries, then added, "I'm going to the veterinary clinic as soon as Jeff and I have breakfast."

"Look, I'm sure that clinic is no place for a boy of Jeff's age. Why don't you let him stay here with me? He and my son always have a good time playing together when Jeff comes to visit you. They can play video games this morning, I'll feed them an early lunch, then we can go to that new community park near the mall. I hear they have all kinds of new playground equipment there. They can burn off some of that boundless energy. I'll have him home by three, and you can spend the day with Hero. I'm sure the boys'll have a good time together."

"The playground, huh? I know Jeff would like that."

"Can I, Aunt Val? Please?"

Valene turned to see a sleepy-faced boy standing behind her, rubbing his eyes. She covered the phone with her hand. "You sure you want to go? I'll be gone most of the day."

He nodded.

She gave him a grin and removed her hand from the receiver. "He says he wants to go. If the offer still stands, and you're sure you want to spend the day with two energetic young boys—"

"Of course I do. It'll be fun."

Val thanked Diane and made arrangements to take Jeff to her condo as soon as he'd had his breakfast. She really wanted to spend some time with Hero, and Diane was right. It would be a depressing experience for Jeff. She grasped the boy by both shoulders and lowered her face to his. "Jeff, you have to promise me to stay with Diane every second. No wandering off, do you hear? And no talking to strangers."

The boy gazed back at her with big, rounded eyes. "I promise, Aunt Val."

The two enjoyed a quick breakfast of hot oatmeal topped with milk and brown sugar, then Valene took Jeff's hand, and they headed for Diane's condo. After handing Diane a piece of paper with the numbers of both her cell phone and the clinic and issuing a few last-minute instructions to Jeff, she started across the lot to her assigned parking space. She'd nearly reached her car when she heard footsteps behind her.

three

Turning quickly, Val found Jordan Young smiling at her in an easy, friendly manner. He was dressed in a pair of jeans and a short-sleeved, pale blue polo shirt that brought out the blue in his eyes.

"Good morning," he chimed out as he approached her. "I hope you slept well. Where's Jeff?"

"He's staying with a neighbor. I kinda hated to take him to the clinic with me."

"Yeah, probably better if he doesn't go. Seeing Hero like that is depressing enough for an adult."

"Well," Valene said, as she pulled her keys from her purse, "I'd better be going."

He stepped between her and her car. "Are you going to the clinic now?"

She nodded.

"My offer still stands. I'd be happy to drive you."

"It'll probably be best if I take my car," she said quickly. "I may want to stay longer than you do."

He shrugged. "I'm not in any hurry. I've got all day."

"I—I need to stop at the store."

"Fine with me. I'm nearly out of coffee."

Valene stood gaping at the man, fresh out of excuses.

"I won't bite."

"I—I know," she mumbled, not sure what to say or do next.

"Aw, come on. Let me drive you there. We're both going to see Hero. Kinda silly to take two vehicles, isn't it? My truck's right there. A mere two spots from yours."

She quickly assessed the situation. Hadn't he taken them right home last night as he'd said he would? Surely, a man who was facing up to his responsibilities as he was could be trusted. "O–okay."

He led her to his Avalanche, opened the door for her, and soon they were headed toward the clinic.

Dr. Bainbridge was standing in the lobby when they arrived. "Good morning."

"Can we see Hero?" Valene asked without returning his greeting.

The veterinarian gave her a warm smile. "I'm sure he'll be glad to see you. I'll be giving him his Rimadyl soon. Once he gets that, he'll be asleep for a number of hours. Don't be alarmed if he seems to be in pain. The effects of last night's pill have worn off, but he'll be fine as soon as this one kicks in. We're keeping him as comfortable as possible."

"Ca–can I stay with him for awhile?"

"We'd both like to stay," Jordan added, stepping up beside her.

The doctor smiled and motioned for them to follow him.

Valene couldn't hold back her gasp when she walked into the little cubicle and found her beloved Hero lying on his side, strapped to a table, completely immobilized. He whined when he saw her and tried to get up, then let out a yelp.

Tears began to roll down her cheeks. "Does he have to be strapped down like that?"

"At this stage, the less he moves around, the better," the doctor explained as he stroked the dog's head. "Why don't you talk to him? Maybe pat his back. I'm sure your presence will have a calming effect on him."

Valene pulled her hair aside and leaned over the whimpering dog. "Shh, Hero. It's okay. I'm here."

Immediately, he calmed down, and his tense body relaxed.

"Looks like you two are good pals." Jordan moved close to her side and carefully wrapped his fingers around one of Hero's front paws. "Hi, Fella."

Hero's pitiful whines tore at Valene's heart, and she had to force herself to keep from sobbing openly.

"I'll come back in a little while and give him his medication," Dr. Bainbridge said. "Meantime, try to keep him calm. We don't want him struggling to get up yet."

"We will," Jordan said, his thumb stroking Hero's paw.

"I know he's in terrible pain," Valene said, wiping her eyes with her sleeve as the door closed behind the kindly doctor. As she lifted her face to Jordan's, she was surprised to find tears in his eyes too.

"He wouldn't even be here, if it weren't for me," he said sadly.

Without thinking, she patted the man's arm reassuringly, knowing the pain he must be experiencing in seeing Hero strapped to the table. "You mustn't feel that way. It was just one of those things that happened. I don't blame you."

Jordan brushed away his tears with the pad of his forefinger. "You probably think I'm a real wimp, but honest, I'd never hurt anyone intentionally."

"I know that." She wanted to slip her arm about his shoulder and comfort him. He seemed so forlorn. "Di—did you ever have a dog?"

"No. My mom wouldn't allow it. She thought dogs were smelly and dirty. But I always wanted one. Is Hero the first dog you've ever had?"

His mother wouldn't allow it? His words surprised her. What mother would deny a boy the joy of having a dog? Gathering her thoughts, Val answered, "No, Vanessa and I had one of those cute little white poodles when we were growing up. We called her Fluff. But I'd always wanted a black Labrador. Hero is special in his own right, but he's extra special since he was a gift from my twin sister. We had a cat too. Ebony."

He grinned. "Ebony?"

She laughed. "Yes. She was sleek with black hair and beautiful squinty eyes. Sorta flirty-like. It seemed the perfect name for her!"

"Yeah, the name Ebony does conjure up that image."

"What kind of dog would you have wanted if you could've had one?"

He tilted his head and pursed his lips thoughtfully. "What kind of dog would I have wanted? Well, to be honest, I don't know. What I really wanted to do was go to the Humane Society and pick out the scroungiest mutt they had. One that looked like he needed a home. Dumb, huh?"

"No, I don't think that's dumb. I think it's sweet. So many animals need homes and someone to love them. I actually thought about going to the Humane Society myself, although I doubt I'd have found a black Lab like Hero. I'd told Vanessa I wanted to get a dog, and being the kind, thoughtful sister she is, she gave me Hero as a gift. He's the best present I could ever have." She lowered herself onto the chair with a grateful smile.

"Well, I think Hero is the perfect name for this magnificent animal. His name fits him well. Like I told you, I've seen you walking him. He has a regal air about him. He looks like a hero."

Valene smiled at her dog. "He is my hero."

"Look how calm he's gotten since you've been here. He's barely moving now, and he's quit whining."

She brightened. "He has calmed down, hasn't he?"

"I'd say, you have a magic touch."

❧

Jordan watched Valene as she wrapped an arm about her

dog and whispered encouragement in his ear. She was pretty, no doubt about it, with her petite, shapely body, her honey-colored hair, and those gorgeous, big blue eyes. But her outward beauty wasn't what impressed him most. He'd been around attractive women all his life. It was her inner beauty. There was a sweet genuineness about her he hadn't seen in most of the women he'd dated, and he found it refreshing. He'd like to know more about Valene Zobel.

"Jordan, would you please get me a tissue from that box on the counter?" she asked, breaking into his thoughts.

"Tissue? Sure." He handed it to her, then watched as she carefully removed a bit of matter from one of Hero's eyes. Her touch was a gentle as a whisper.

"There," she said, tossing the tissue into a big metal wastebasket. "You're a good doggie."

With a slight yelp, Hero shifted his front legs, but Valene was quick to place a hand on him. "Stay still, Hero."

"He's a lucky dog."

She turned toward Jordan. "Lucky?"

"To have someone who cares for him like you do."

She grinned. "You're here too. You must care."

"I do care. It's killing me to see him looking so forlorn, knowing I'm the one who caused his injuries."

"Jordan, you're a wonderful man. I want you to know how much I appreciate you and your interest in Hero. You didn't have to come here. I'm sure you have more pleasant things to do than spend your morning at an animal hospital."

"I'm wonderful? I nearly ran over your nephew, and I hit your dog! I don't call that wonderful."

"Enough of that."

He felt her hand on his arm. "Okay. You win. I'm wonderful."

Valene laughed. "Yes, you are. Learn to live with it."

He snickered. "If I'm so wonderful, how about letting me take you to lunch after the doc gives Hero his medicine? I know this great little Italian restaurant down on Clifton Boulevard. Their specialty is pollo alla cacciatora. And you'll love their garlic bread. Only problem is, you can't breathe on anyone for a week after you eat it without them passing out!"

He watched as she laughed and seemed to be considering his invitation, hoping she'd accept. "Aw, come on, say yes. You've already told me Jeff won't be home until three."

Before she could answer, Dr. Bainbridge came in, carrying Hero's pill on a small plastic tray.

"Well, looks like having you here is better than medicine. I'm amazed Hero is this calm, considering his Rimadyl has worn off."

They watched as Dr. Bainbridge skillfully maneuvered the tablet down the dog's throat. Although Hero fought him a bit and tried to struggle, the doctor held him fast, and soon the dog swallowed the pill with very little difficulty.

"It won't take too long before he'll be getting sleepy," the doctor said with a gentle tap to Hero's nose. "He'll probably be out for several hours. If he gets along okay, you should be able to take him home in three or four days."

"Can I stay until he goes to sleep?" Valene asked quickly.

"You can stay as long as you like," Dr. Bainbridge answered. "It's obvious Hero likes having you here."

As soon as the doctor shut the door behind him, Valene turned to Jordan. "You don't have to stay. I can take a taxi home."

"Valene, you have to eat. We'll both stay until Hero goes to sleep; then I want to take you to lunch. Please. Buying you a meal is the least I can do."

"Well, I'm not sure, I—"

"Please?"

"Umm, I guess, but I'll pay for my own lunch."

He smiled. She'd said yes. "We'll argue about that later."

Nearly twenty minutes passed before Hero fell into a deep sleep. Jordan's heart was touched as he watched Valene bend over the sleeping dog and whisper something in his ear. He knew she was hurting, and he wanted to take her in his arms and comfort her. There was something so sweet and innocent about her that surprisingly tugged at his heartstrings. But he also knew, since they were barely acquainted, his comfort could only come from words. "He'll be fine," he told her, reaching out his hand.

"I know. I'm being an old worrywart. But he's important to me. I can't imagine life without him. I'm also a fraidy-cat. There's no way I could sleep nights without Hero by my side." Although she ignored Jordan's hand, she gave him a smile.

"A beautiful woman can't be too careful these days." He pulled the door open, catching the delicate scent of her perfume as she moved past him.

"Look, it was nice of you to volunteer to help with Hero, but it's really not necessary. I'll manage somehow."

"Oh, but it is necessary. I would never forgive myself if I didn't help you. After all—"

She put a finger to his lips. "No blame game, remember?"

"Then you'll accept my help?" he asked as he pushed open the outer door.

"Maybe. We'll see."

The restaurant was crowded, but after a twenty-minute wait, they were escorted to a table in the far back corner. Jordan smiled at his luncheon guest over the menu. There was something about her that held him spellbound. Was it her smile? Her beautiful eyes? Or could it be her gentle ways? He couldn't be sure exactly what attracted him to her, but he found himself wanting to spend more time with Valene.

"What did you say was their specialty?"

"Ah, the pollo alla cacciatora? I think you'll like it."

She nodded. "Then that's what I'll have. If you say it's good, I'm sure it is."

When the waitress came to take their order, Jordan handed her their menus and ordered for both of them. "Thanks for coming with me," he told Valene once the waitress had moved on. "I hate eating alone."

She let out a slight sigh. "Me too. Before Nathan and Vanessa started dating, she and I always had lunch together. Now I have to eat alone."

"You love your sister very much, don't you?"

She nodded. "Yes, I do. But she's Nathan's now."

"You make her sound like a possession."

She frowned. "I do, don't I? She's anything but a possession. My sister is her own person. She's the strong one, the leader. I've always been the follower."

"Funny, you don't impress me as a follower," he said, meaning it. "From what I've observed in our short time together, I'd say you're very strong in your own right."

"Really? You think so?"

"Really."

"Everyone loves Vanessa," she went on. "She has what you call a sparkling personality. She's terrific."

"So are you." He almost wished he hadn't made that comment when she turned to him with a frown, but he couldn't help himself. She was terrific, and not at all like most of the women he knew. They were much more interested in themselves than in others. Valene impressed him as one who always put other's interests ahead of her own.

"You're only saying that because you haven't met my sister."

"I'm saying it because I've met you."

The waitress brought their drinks, a basket of hot onion-garlic rolls, and a plate of butter squares.

"These rolls are best when you slather them with butter." He offered the basket to her.

"Don't tempt me, Jordan," she said, hesitating before taking a roll from the basket. "I love butter, but I'm trying to keep my fat grams down to a reasonable number."

"You don't know what you're missing. Better try it."

"I will, in a second."

He watched as Valene bowed her head. He knew she was praying, but he couldn't help staring at her. It was as if praying was a natural part of her life.

When she lifted her head, she spread a pat of butter onto her roll. "Umm, you're right. These are delicious and well worth the extra grams of fat."

"Told you so."

The two of them sat smiling at each other as they consumed their rolls. When their lunch arrived, Jordan grinned with satisfaction as Valene took her first bite of the pollo alla cacciatora.

"Umm, it's fabulous."

"Are you glad you came?" He hoped this would be the first of many times they'd dine together.

She ducked her head shyly and gave him a demure smile. "Yes, but I do feel a bit guilty having such a wonderful lunch when poor Hero is barely able to eat."

"Valene, Hero is in good hands," he reminded her. "He's probably sleeping right now and doesn't even realize you're gone."

She nodded. "I know, but. . ."

"If anyone should feel guilty, it's me. I'm the one—"

She lifted her palms to him. "I'm sorry, Jordan. I know I'm

being foolish, but Hero is much more than a pet. He's my companion. My roommate."

He reached out his hand, palm up. "Let's make a pact. No more sad talk while we're enjoying our lunch. Okay?"

She placed her hand in his. "Okay, no more sad talk."

He knew he should let go, but he didn't want to and held on to her hand longer than he should. When Valene finally pulled it away, he smiled awkwardly. "It's nice to have company. Thanks for coming."

"Thanks for inviting me."

"You were a tough sell. I wasn't sure I was going to be able to convince you to come with me."

"I–I nearly didn't."

"I'm glad you did."

"Me too."

"Well, if it isn't Jordan Young!"

At the sound of a woman's voice, both Jordan and Valene looked up into the gorgeous face of a tall, willowy blond.

four

Jordan rose quickly. "Charmaine. Hello!"

"Where've you been keeping yourself, Jordie? It's been weeks since I've heard from you." The woman's words fairly dripped with honey.

"I–I've been busy." He gestured toward Valene. "Charmaine King, this is Valene Zobel."

The woman gave her a cool, indifferent stare.

"Hello, Ms. King. It's nice to meet you."

As quickly as she'd looked in Valene's direction, the blond turned away. "Jordie, Dear, I'm giving a dinner party Saturday night at the country club. I do hope you can come. I've missed you. All your friends will be there."

"Sorry, Charmaine. I'm going to be busy all weekend. But thanks for the invitation."

The look on the woman's face said she didn't like being turned down. "All weekend?"

"Long story." He shot a glance at Valene. "Some other time, perhaps."

Charmaine started to say something but stopped. She sent an icy stare Valene's way.

"I'll call you sometime," Jordan told the attractive woman, none too enthusiastically.

Charmaine gave him a coquettish smile as she ran a well-manicured fingernail down his arm. "I think that's what you said the last time we talked, but I never heard from you. You do have my phone number, don't you?"

"Like I said, Charmaine, I've been busy, and yes, I'm sure I have your number somewhere."

"Maybe we can play a game of tennis or take in a movie."

Jordan nodded. "Maybe."

Charmaine seemed a bit perturbed by his nonchalance. "Well, I'll leave you two to your lunch. Nice to have met you, Virginia."

"Valene," Jordan said, correcting her.

She shot an uninterested glance Valene's way. "Oh, yes. Valene." Then she smiled at him and, adding more honey to her words, added, "I'll be waiting for your call, Jordie."

"Good-bye, Charmaine." Jordan sat back down and grinned sheepishly at Valene. "Sorry about that."

"You needn't be sorry. It's always nice to see old friends." She grinned back. "I got the feeling she was quite happy to see you."

"More coffee?" he asked, changing the subject, which was fine with her. However, she couldn't get the woman off her mind. Her gorgeous tanned figure, her beautifully coifed hair, her expensive clothing, all spelled wealth. Was this Charmaine person one of Jordan's girlfriends?

What business was it of hers? She wouldn't even be with the man if he hadn't hit her dog. That was his only interest in her. There was no way a handsome man like Jordan Young would choose her as his luncheon guest unless the two of them had been thrown together under such unusual circumstances.

"How about dessert?" Jordan asked as the waitress cleared away their dishes. "Spumoni ice cream!"

Valene shook her head as she placed a hand on her abdomen. "I'm too full to even think about it. Besides, I want to get back to Hero, and I'm sure you have plans."

"My only plan is to take you back to the vet's, spend time with Hero, and get you home before Jeff gets back."

"But—"

"Sorry, Valene. You're stuck with me."

After spending another hour with Hero, Valene and Jordan drove back to her condo.

"Wanna ride in the morning?" he asked, as he stopped the truck in front of her place. "I heard the doc tell you it'd be okay to visit Hero, even if it is Sunday."

She shook her head. "Thanks for the offer, but I'll be at church in the morning. I'll probably head over to see Hero after I have lunch with my parents."

His brows lifted as he leaped from the truck and rushed around to open her door. "Oh? Your parents live around here?"

"Yes, in Granite Cliff, if you can call about fifteen miles away, 'around here.' I still go to Seaside Chapel, our home church in Granite Cliff, even though I live here in Spring Valley." She slipped out of the seat and waited while he closed the door. "Do you go to church?"

"Me? Yeah, I usually make the early service, unless I need to be at the base."

"Then you're a Christian?"

He nodded and stuck his hands in his pockets, rattling his change. "When I was about ten, I went to my friend's church for some special meeting. They had this missionary speak, and he was pretty good. I went to the front of the church at the end of the service and accepted God into my life."

Valene brightened. Jordan is a Christian?

"I really meant it at the time," he went on, "but when I got home and told my dad, he said Christianity was nothing but a bunch of do-good, confused people." He grinned and wiggled his eyebrows. "I confess it made me question my decision. But when I was about fifteen and went to a youth meeting, I learned more about the Bible, and I knew I'd made the right decision despite my dad's ridicule. How about you?"

"I asked God to come into my life when I was about that age."

"Like I said, I meant it at the time, but I was too young to really understand, and there was never anyone around to explain things to me. But I'm sure God heard that little ten-year-old boy's prayers."

"I'm sure He did."

Jordan looked off in space, as if avoiding her eyes. "I'm not as close to God as I should be."

She wondered at his words but decided it was best not to ask for an explanation. "You should visit my church sometime. The music is fabulous."

"Maybe I will, if you invite me."

Valene felt her heart skip a beat. "We even have an orchestra. I love the music."

"Personally, I like country music."

"Oh, I've got some great Southern Gospel CDs you'd like," she told him with enthusiasm.

"I'd like that." Although he smiled, she detected a note of sadness in his voice.

"I'll loan you some, if you promise to listen to them." She pulled her keys from her purse and handed them to him. He took them with a grin, and the two walked to her door.

"After the early service, I'm gonna run by the vet's and check on Hero. I have plans for tomorrow afternoon, so I guess I won't be seeing you until Monday." He unlocked her door, pushed it open, and handed her keys back to her. "Maybe, by then, Dr. Bainbridge can tell us when you can bring Hero home, and we can work out a schedule."

She gave him a blank stare. "A schedule?"

"Sure. The doc said Hero's going to need constant care, twenty-four/seven. You can't do that alone. I told you

I'd help."

"I know you did, but I really didn't expect you to go through with it."

He leaned his lanky body against the door jam and smiled. "Hey, I don't say things I don't mean. Like I told the doc, I aim to do my part."

She ducked past him and stood in the open doorway, feeling as tongue-tied as a schoolgirl on her first date. "We'll see."

"I'll call you tomorrow night."

"Okay." She pushed the door almost shut, then stood watching him through the crack. Jordan Young was the kind of man most women only dreamed about. He'd barely stepped away from the door when his cell phone rang. Valene knew she shouldn't eavesdrop, but she listened anyway, assuming it was one of his many girlfriends. Maybe even that obnoxious Charmaine person.

Jordan quickly pulled the cell phone from his belt. "Hello," he said as he tugged out the little antenna. "Yes, I can make it by five. No problem. I don't mind a bit."

She watched as he hurried to his truck and pulled into his parking place. Who was he meeting at five o'clock? *It's none of your business, dummy.*

Jeff arrived home right at three and chattered a mile a minute about the park Diane had taken them to. Val loved the way his face beamed with enthusiasm as he talked. When Vanessa and Nathan had first asked her to baby-sit Jeff while they were on their honeymoon, she'd been a bit apprehensive. Jeff had been to visit her with Vanessa before but had never actually spent the night. She found she enjoyed having him around. The two got along quite well.

"I hope you thanked Diane for taking you," she finally said

when she could get a word in.

"I did, Aunt Val, and she said she'd take me again sometime."

She smiled at her nephew. "I told Hero why you didn't come and visit him today. He was a bit sleepy while I was there, but he's doing fine. Mr. Young was there too."

"I like him. He's nice."

"Yes, he is nice."

Jeff hurried off to watch one of his Saturday afternoon cartoon shows while Valene put a load in the washer. She added the soap to the dispenser, and had just hit the on button, when the doorbell rang. She hurried into the little foyer and, after peeking through the peephole, flung open the door.

There, standing on her porch, was Jordan Young, and he was wearing a naval flight suit.

"You left your scarf in my truck. I thought you might need it." He reached the colorful scarf toward her.

She took it but stood gaping at him. "You're in the navy?"

He grinned. "No, I'm on my way to a Halloween party."

She suddenly realized how stupid she sounded. Of course, he was in the navy. Why else would he be wearing a naval flight suit?

He pounded his forehead with his palm. "That wasn't a very nice thing for me to say. You'll have to excuse me. Sometimes I speak before I think." His smile was quite congenial. "I'm stationed at the San Diego Base. I'm a navy pilot. I fly the F-18 Hornet. You know, one of those planes that lands on aircraft carriers. I was supposed to be off all weekend, but a buddy called and asked me to file some reports for him. His wife has gone into premature labor."

"I—I'm sorry. I didn't mean to stare. It's just—well, we've never talked about our occupations. I—"

"Guess we didn't, did we? I don't even know what you do."

She shrugged. "My occupation isn't really a career. It's simply a job. I work in medical records at Community Hospital. I haven't decided what I want to be when I grow up."

He laughed, and she once again felt at ease.

"I never had that problem. I've planned on being a navy pilot from the time I was old enough to know what one was. My dad served in the navy too. My plan was to see the world before I settled down, just like he did. I've already seen a great deal of it. There's so much out there to see and do. Being a navy pilot gives me a chance to do just that, and I'm going to take advantage of every opportunity I can."

"You're lucky. I graduated college with a degree in marketing, which means I'm qualified for everything and nothing. I'm surprised you have a condo here. Couldn't you live on the base?"

"Yep, but when we're in port and not out on a mission, I prefer to have a place off-base too. That way, I can stay here when I have free time and on weekends. I prefer my privacy, and an abundance of entertainment and sports activities, not to mention a variety of good restaurants. Sure beats the base's elbow-to-elbow camaraderie, mainly military-centered activities, and base chow."

She snickered. "Isn't it scary to land on one of those ships? I've seen them do it on the news. I can't imagine being in a plane caught by its tail hook on a cable."

"I gotta admit, I've done it hundreds of times in my ten years with the navy, but the old adrenalin starts pumpin' each time I do it. I wouldn't give it up for anything." He sent her a grin as he backed away. "Well, I'd better scoot. I want to be at the base by five."

"Ah. . .sure. Thanks for returning the scarf."

"You're welcome. Say a little prayer for me when you go to church."

"I—I will."

Again, she closed the door all but a crack and watched as the handsome, uniformed man climbed into his truck and sped off. "Wow," she said aloud as she closed the door. "Does he ever look great in that uniform."

⁂

Val's mother was waiting on the church steps when she and Jeff arrived the next morning. After making sure Jeff made it to the right Sunday school classroom, the two of them sat down on one of the sofas in the welcome center.

"I couldn't believe it when you called and told me about Jeff and that bicycle. I'd told your sister he should leave it at our house, but he insisted on taking it with him, and you know how she wants to please him." Her face filled with concern. "How's Hero?"

"Oh, Mom, you should've seen him. He was lying so still. I was sure he was dead, but Jordan rushed him to the vet's, and—"

"Jordan? Is that the man who hit him?"

"Yes, he's been wonderful. I don't think I could've gotten through this whole ordeal without him."

"He should be wonderful to you! Racing that truck of his through a parking lot—"

"No! It wasn't like that. He wasn't driving fast at all. I'd told Jeff to stay on the sidewalk. He disobeyed me. If Jordan hadn't hit the brake pedal when he did. . ."

Her mother grabbed her wrist. "Oh, Valene, don't even say it!"

Valene turned her face away and blinked back tears. "I should never have let Hero out without his leash. Now he's lying in the clinic with a fractured pelvis."

"Do—do you think perhaps it would've been better for him, if you'd—"

"Put him to sleep? No! I would never do that!"

"But, Dear, do you have any idea how much his veterinarian and hospital bills will be? And how much care he's going to require? Can you handle all of that?"

"Jordan is paying all his bills, and he's volunteered to help me take care of him."

"He is?"

"Yes, Mother, he is. He's the most honorable, responsible man I've ever met."

"Oh, Valene, I worry about you. You're not strong like your sister. Please don't take on more than you can handle."

Jordan's words rang in Valene's mind. *Funny, you don't impress me as a follower. From what I've observed in our short time together, I'd say you're very strong in your own right.* "Perhaps I'm stronger than you think."

"Just be careful. You don't really know this man."

"I trust him, Mom."

"Are you sure you don't want Jeff to spend the week with us?"

"No, I've taken off the entire week. He'll be fine. I told Vanessa I'd take care of him. I'll be bringing Hero home probably Tuesday or Wednesday, and he can help me with him during the day. I think Jordan will be helping at night."

"Promise me you'll be careful."

"I will."

❧

"Time to go," Valene called out to Jeff after a pleasant lunch and a leisurely visit with her parents. "I know you're having a great time playing with Lick, but we want to spend some time with Hero."

Jeff wrapped his arms about his dog and gave him a big squeeze. "Sorry, Lick, but I gotta go see your brother. He can't run and play like you can, and I think he's lonely."

"We'll take good care of him," Valene's mother assured the boy, patting him on the shoulder. "You'll be back with him next week, but right now I think your Aunt Valene needs you."

Jeff gave his dog one more squeeze, then bounded toward the door with Lick at his heels. "Okay."

~

When Valene and her new nephew arrived back at the condo after spending some time with Hero, they played a game of Clue, then put on one of her favorite CDs while Jeff showed her how he could do somersaults across the living-room floor. They enjoyed hot dogs at a nearby drive-in, then stopped by the video store and rented a movie.

She fixed them tall glasses of fresh lemonade, popped the videotape in the VCR, and the two settled themselves on the sofa to watch the movie. She had to smile as she straightened the cover on the armrest, remembering how she and Vanessa and their friends had struggled, getting that sofa from their old apartment to her new condo. She'd bought it second-hand, but it still looked good. The pale blue upholstery was as lovely as when she'd seen it that first time.

Occasionally, Valene would glance at the phone. When it finally rang, she grabbed the receiver on the first ring and tugged it into the hall, where she could talk without disturbing Jeff, who was engrossed in the movie. As she'd hoped, it was Jordan.

"Hi," she said, trying not to sound too eager. "How'd your day go?"

"Fine. It was just routine. How about yours?"

She smiled into the phone. "It was good. Jeff and I went to church, had lunch with my folks, visited Hero for an hour or so, then came home. He's watching a movie."

"That's it?"

"Well, we did start an exciting game of Clue."

He let out a chuckle. "Who did it? Colonel Mustard in the library, using a candlestick?"

She laughed. "How'd you guess?"

"I've played that game hundreds of times. Why do kids like that thing?"

"I don't know. My sister and I played it too. I used to think it was exciting when I was little, but I had a hard time gathering up any enthusiasm to play it with Jeff. He enjoyed it, though, and that made it bearable."

"Did you pray for me?"

His question took her aback. "Ye—yes, I did."

"Hey, thanks. I wondered why things went so well today."

She laughed. "Then I'll pray for you again tomorrow."

"I have an early morning meeting, so I'm going to stay on the base tonight, but I should be back to Spring Valley by four. What time are you going to go see Hero?"

"I thought I'd go in the morning. Jeff's going with me."

"Oh."

She detected a tinge of disappointment in his voice. "Diane said she'd keep him if I wanted to go back later."

"About four?"

"Probably." Her heart raced.

"Wanna ride?"

"Yes, that would be very nice. I hate driving in late-afternoon traffic."

"I'll try to make it by four. Don't leave without me."

"I won't."

"Valene."

"Yes?"

"Nothing. See you at four."

She cradled the phone in her hand long after the connection had been severed. What had he started to say?

❧

"Hey, Young! Wanna get a beer with us?" two of Jordan's squad members asked as the three of them walked along.

He shifted his briefcase to his other hand. "No, thanks. I have a four o'clock appointment, and I have to drive to my condo."

"A blond appointment?" one of them asked with a wink.

Jordan felt himself blushing. "Actually, I'm going to visit a dog in the animal hospital."

One of the men elbowed him as they walked along. "Aw, you don't expect us to believe that, do you? Come on, you can tell us. Who is she?"

"Honest, fellas, I'm going to visit a dog!"

"Give her a kiss for us, will you?"

He waved good-bye, then strode off in the direction of the parking lot. *Give her a kiss for you? I'd like to give her a kiss for me!*

It was exactly 3:55 when Jordan arrived at Valene's condo. She was waiting for him on the little bench on her porch. "You're early," she called out as he exited his pickup.

"I knew you were waiting for me. Ready?"

"You bet." She crawled into the truck as he held the door open for her.

He hurried around to the driver's side and slid under the steering wheel. "How was Hero this morning?"

"Pathetic."

The smile left his face. "He's not doing well?"

"I didn't say that. I said he was pathetic. All those places where he skidded on the pavement have turned crusty, and he's beginning to try to move around a bit more. It breaks my heart to see him like that."

"I know," he said softly as the Avalanche moved out of the lot and onto the street. "He's been on my mind constantly.

I wish I could trade places with him."

"Somehow," she said, her frown turning to a smile, "I can't imagine you barking and eating dog biscuits."

"Aw, you know what I mean."

"I know. I wish I could trade places with him too."

"Did the vet say when you could take him home?"

"Wednesday."

His face brightened. "Really? Good. I know I can get someone to cover for me Wednesday. That way, I'll be able to help you with him."

Valene felt a sense of relief. She'd had no idea how she was going to manage bringing the big dog home by herself. "I'd really appreciate the help, if you're sure it won't inconvenience you."

"No trouble at all. I'm one of the few single guys in my unit. A lot of the married men owe me time for covering for them."

As they entered the clinic, Valene felt Jordan's hand on the small of her back, and his touch sent chills up her spine.

"Ah, I'm glad to see you both," Dr. Bainbridge told them as they entered the waiting room. "That dog of yours is determined to get up. I think it's time we let him."

The three of them made their way to the little cubicle where Hero still lay strapped to a table about two feet wide and nearly twice his length.

"Ms. Zobel," the doctor said, reaching out a long piece of terry cloth, "when Mr. Young lifts Hero, you and I are going to slip this cloth beneath him, directly in front of your dog's hind legs, okay?"

Valene nodded.

"Okay, Mr. Young. Wrap your arms around Hero's midsection and lift him on the count of three. And be prepared. This is going to hurt him, but it has to be done if he's going to get his strength back." He gestured toward Valene. "Ready, Ms. Zobel? One. Two. Three. Lift!"

Each did their job, and with only one loud yelp, Hero's hind end was lifted and supported by the makeshift sling.

"Steady, Boy," the vet said, tugging up on one end of the cloth. "He won't be able to stand on his own, but he'll be encouraged. It's his natural instinct to want to stand despite the pain he's experiencing."

Valene wanted to cover her ears. The pitiful sounds coming from Hero as he struggled to stand were almost more than she could bear. A quick glance at Jordan confirmed that Hero's obvious pain was getting to him too.

Dr. Bainbridge gestured toward Hero. "It's time for his Rimadyl, but I wanted him totally alert the first time we tried this. We'll let him struggle for a few minutes, then we'll lay him back over on his side, and I'll give him his medication."

Neither Valene nor Jordan seemed to think of anything to say. They just watched the helpless dog make his futile efforts. Eventually, the doctor motioned for them to lower him.

"Now I want to show you how to exercise him. Each of you grab onto one end again while I assist Hero. As he tries to drag himself forward, we're going to help him by tugging slowly on the cloth. He won't get far, but with you taking some of the strain off his hind end and his skeletal frame and muscles, it will relieve his pain somewhat. When you take him home, this is what you'll have to do to help him learn to maneuver again. Do you think you can handle it?"

They both nodded.

"Okay, pull."

Valene winced when Hero let out another painful sounding moan.

"Like I told you, it's going to get messy. He won't be able to take care of his bodily functions like he would if he were outside. You'll have to clean up after him until that pelvis heals and he's able to walk around by himself."

"We'll do whatever is necessary," Jordan said without hesitation, and somehow Valene knew he meant it. She wouldn't have to face this alone.

They watched as Hero stood on his front legs and tried to pull his back legs to a standing position, but it was impossible, even with their help.

"It'll come, Boy. Just be patient," Dr. Bainbridge said as he again patted Hero's head. "That old adage is true. No pain, no gain. It's true for dogs as well as humans."

"He—he's so helpless," Valene said, her voice cracking with emotion.

"Ah, but he has you!" Dr. Bainbridge gave her a compassionate smile. "Not all dogs have owners who are as patient and as willing to work with them and nurse them back to health. After seeing you two and the love you both seem to have for this dog, I have no doubt he's going to be up and running around in no time."

"We won't desert him, Doc," Jordan added, seeming to speak for both of them.

They allowed Hero another three full minutes on his front feet before the doctor said he'd had enough for one day. Within thirty minutes of taking his medication, the dog was once again stretched out on the table, strapped down, and fast asleep. Valene bent and kissed the tip of his ear before whispering, "Good night."

When she stood, she found Jordan staring at her. The look in his eyes told her he was as concerned about Hero as she was, and she was thankful. If Hero had to be hit by a truck, she was grateful he was hit by someone who cared and who faced up to his responsibility. That's exactly what Jordan Young was doing.

"Are you ready to go?" he asked softly, as if he didn't want to disturb the sleeping dog.

She smiled up into his kind face. "Yes. I'm ready."

As they moved out toward the parking lot, she felt Jordan's hand once again go to the small of her back. The same chill ran up her spine.

"How are we going to work this out?" he asked once they had turned toward home.

"You mean our schedule?"

He nodded as he sent a quick glance her way. "I'll try to be available any time you need me, but I figured the nights might be best. That way, you could get a good night's sleep."

She paused as she thought things over. "I knew it was going to be tough, but I didn't know how tough until this afternoon. I'm not sure what would be best."

"Maybe you could call me each time Hero needs to be moved. And I don't mind cleaning him up," he inserted quickly. "I'll take the night shift too."

She frowned. "How would that work? He's too heavy to move back and forth from my condo to yours. We don't want to cause him any more pain than necessary."

He let out a long, low sigh. "I hadn't thought of that."

"I know!" she said excitedly. "I can take next week off too! I've been working a lot of overtime the past few months— there has been so much sickness in our department. Instead of my usual ten-hour-a-day, four-day workweek, some weeks I've been working as many as six days. I know I have at least five or six days of comp time coming. Maybe more. This would be the perfect time to use them."

"That'd sure help," he said, "but what about the night thing? You can't take care of him all day and all night too."

Her enthusiasm waned. "I guess we have plenty of time to work something out. He won't be coming home until

Wednesday." *But what? I can't have a near-stranger spending the nights in my condo. Maybe he can take the day shift, and I'll take nights. But that wouldn't work. It wouldn't be proper for him to spend his days taking care of Hero while I'm sleeping in the other room. Then there's Jeff to consider. He'll be with me until Saturday, when he goes over to Mom and Dad's to stay until Vanessa and Nathan get back from their honeymoon. And I have to go back to work after next week. What'll I do with Hero while I'm at work and Jordan is at the base?*

"Yeah," he said, scratching his head as if he, too, were deliberating their dilemma. "We probably need to give it some more thought."

"Yes, I guess we do."

"I'm sure we'll find an answer that's workable for both of us," he said confidently.

They rode along in silence for several blocks. Valene's mind was a blank. The situation seemed impossible, yet they had to come up with a workable solution.

"I don't know about you, but I think better with food in my stomach. Why don't we call and have pizza delivered to your condo? I'm sure Jeff would like it, and I hate—"

"To eat alone," she said, finishing his sentence.

"Exactly."

"But, Jordan, you've done so much already."

He glanced at her, taking his eyes off the road for only a second. "Not nearly as much as I'd like to."

She meditated over his comment before answering, wondering exactly what he meant. "Okay, but if you do this, you have to allow me to fix supper tomorrow night. Nothing fancy, but that way we can devote our full attention to Hero. Providing you're still willing to help me bring him home."

"Of course, I am!" He pulled his cell phone off his belt and handed it to her with a grin. "Hit six on the speed dial.

That's the pizza phone number. I call it often. Order whatever you and Jeff would like. Me? I like it all."

"How about a large, half supreme, half pepperoni?"

"Sounds great."

When they arrived at the condo, Valene opened things up while Jordan went to Diane's to retrieve Jeff. By the time they'd returned, she had poured soda for them and set paper plates and napkins on the coffee table. "I thought we'd eat our pizza in here."

"Pizza? Kewl!" Jeff said in exaggerated tones. "I love pizza. Me and my dad eat it all the time."

"Pepperoni okay, Sport?" Jordan asked as he sat down on the sofa and stretched his arms wide across its back.

"My favorite," Jeff said, sitting down beside him.

Jordan looked around the room. "Nice condo. I like the way you have it fixed. It looks like you."

She gave him a shy grin. "Is that a compliment? Other than the second-hand sofa, it's mostly garage-sale stuff."

"Are you renting your condo, or did you buy?"

"I bought it. I hated to pay rent and have nothing to show for it at the end of the year. My grandparents left my sister and me some money. She wisely bought the pet shop where we'd worked, and renamed it Whiskers, Wags, and Wings. Cute name, huh? Vanessa has always been the creative one."

"And you bought your condo?"

She nodded. "I figured any property in the San Diego area was a good investment. I hope I was right."

"I hope you were too. That's the main reason I bought my condo. I like this complex."

Jordan leaped from the sofa when the doorbell rang, paid for the pizza, and gave the delivery boy an overly generous tip.

He placed the pizza box on the table. "I suppose you're going to want to pray over this, right?"

"You mind?"

He shook his head. "Of course not."

"I wanna pray," Jeff said, surprising Valene.

She gave him a smile. "Sure, Jeff. Go ahead."

"Dear Lord. Thanks for the pizza and Aunt Valene and Mr. Young and Hero. And thanks for the doctor who is going to make him well. Be with my daddy and my new mama and with Lick too. Amen."

"Hey, that's pretty good," Jordan told him with a laugh. "Better'n I do."

Jeff gave him a quizzical look. "I talk to God all the time. Don't you ever talk to Him?"

Valene muffled a snicker. Leave it to a kid to get right to the point.

Jordan frowned. "Oh, I pray to Him alright, Jeff. But sometimes, I'm not sure God wants to hear from me."

Jeff shrugged with childlike innocence. "God wants to hear from everyone."

Jordan tousled the boy's hair. "Let's dig into this pizza before it gets cold."

A red flag went up in Valene's thoughts. Whatever did Jordan mean?

Valene and Jordan consumed the supreme half of the pizza, while Jeff worked on the pepperoni half.

"I'm stuffed." Jordan leaned back into the sofa and rubbed his stomach. "How about you, Sport?"

Jeff grinned. "Me too."

Valene rose and began gathering plates, napkins, and glasses and placing them on her tray. "While you two boys relax, I'll take this stuff into the kitchen and take care of the leftovers."

Jordan stood quickly and grabbed onto the tray. "No, I'll do it. You relax."

They stood staring at one another, each wearing a challenging smile.

Valene let go of the tray and motioned him toward the kitchen. "We'll both do it."

She led the way and he followed.

"This has been nice," he said as he placed the tray on the counter. "Thanks for letting me stay."

"Thank you for the pizza."

"Maybe we can do it again after we bring Hero home."

She smiled over her shoulder as she placed their glasses and silverware in the dishwasher. "Maybe."

"I guess I'd better be going. I've got another early morning meeting scheduled with my work crew, but I'll be home about four. I could drive you to see Hero again. Maybe Jeff'll want to come along this time."

"I'd like that. Are you sure it won't inconvenience you?"

"Not at all. I want to drive you. I like being with you."

She felt herself blushing. She liked being with him too, but she'd never tell him.

He leaned down and planted a quick kiss on her cheek. "See you about four tomorrow."

His sudden kiss rendered her speechless. "I. . .ah. . .yes, four. See you then."

She watched as he strode down her sidewalk and turned toward his condo. *Oh, dear Lord. I think I'm falling in love. Jordan is everything I could ever want in a man. But why would he ever want me?*

She and Jeff watched a skateboard special on TV, then worked a few puzzles in the workbook she'd bought him when they'd gone shopping. "Off to bed with you," she told him, as she closed the book and placed it on the coffee table.

"Do I have to go to bed now, Aunt Valene?"

She nodded. "Your dad gave me strict instructions for you

to be in bed by nine. Don't forget to brush your teeth."

Valene smiled as she watched the boy pad off toward the bathroom. Someday she'd like to have children.

She pulled the toss pillows off the sofa and began making out a bed for Jeff. She was just putting the quilt in place when she heard a soft rapping sound. After a quick look through the peephole, she opened the door.

five

"I've got it!" Jordan called out excitedly as his hands grasped her shoulders.

"You've got what?"

"The way we can take care of Hero when he comes home! I was getting ready for bed when it hit me!"

She couldn't help but smile. He must've been serious about getting ready for bed when he was struck by inspiration. He had on a simple white T-shirt and a pair of khaki shorts and was barefoot. "So, what's this plan of yours?"

"You can stay at my condo!"

"Stay at your condo? I don't understand. Why would I want to do that?"

"Look, I've got it all planned out. It'd be much too difficult to move Hero from place to place, right?"

She nodded.

"So, until you go back to work, you stay with him days while I'm at work. I'll be home about four, and I'll come over and help you exercise him. Then, when it's your bedtime, you can go over to my condo and spend the night. That way, you'll get a good night's sleep, and I can take care of Hero!"

She gave him a frown. "But when are you going to sleep?"

"With the lights out, he'll probably sleep most of the night. But when he needs help or needs to be cleaned up, I'll be there to take care of him. I'll wake you up when it's time for me to leave in the morning."

His enthusiasm overwhelmed her. "But, Jordan, don't you

see? You're getting the worst end of that plan. I couldn't let you do such an unselfish thing."

"Nothing unselfish about it. I owe it to you and that terrific dog of yours. Besides, it'll give me an excuse to spend the evenings with you. Maybe we can even have supper together again."

She didn't know what to say and just stared at him.

"Think about it. It's a good plan." He bent and kissed her on the forehead. "Now, you'd better get some sleep. Good night, sweet lady."

"Ah. . .good night."

Valene stood holding onto the knob even after she'd closed the door. Jordan had kissed her. Twice! Her fingers rose to touch her forehead. *Be still, my heart. It was only a friendly gesture. He meant nothing by it. If it weren't for Hero, he wouldn't take a second look at me. Vanessa, maybe. But not me!*

☙

By four o'clock the next day, Val was a basket case. All she'd been able to think about was Jordan Young. Even Jeff had noticed her spaced-out look and had asked her about it. She'd awkwardly explained she was merely concerned about Hero, which she was.

She raced to open the door when Jordan arrived.

"Ready?" he asked.

She nodded and gave him a warm smile. "Come on, Jeff," she called. "It's time to go see Hero."

"Shut the door and make sure it locks," Jordan told Jeff over his shoulder as he led Valene to his pickup. Once they reached it, Jordan took Valene's hand in his. "Let me help you. I don't think they designed these Avalanches for women wearing skirts."

She let out a giggle. "I guess not." The warmth of his hand on hers made her heart sing. *Down, Girl. He only took your hand to assist you. Nothing more. Don't read things that aren't there. You'll only set yourself up for disappointment.*

"So, how was Hero when you visited him today?" he asked as she settled into the smooth leather seat.

"The doctor said he's doing as well as could be expected, but I don't know. Hero's trying to move around even more, and it's so obvious he's in pain. It hurts me to see him that way."

"I know, and tomorrow it'll be up to us to help him move around. Think you can handle it?"

"I have to handle it. I don't have a choice, if I want to see him get well."

He closed her door, checked to make sure Jeff was secure in his seat belt and that the door was shut tight, then hurried around to the other side.

"It's very kind of you to drive us to the vet's," Val told him, wanting him to know how much she appreciated it.

"Yeah, I like to ride in your Avalanche!" Jeff chimed in from the backseat. "It's kewl. Wish my dad had one."

"Avalanche? That's what you call this truck?" Valene asked, searching the dash for a brand name.

"Aunt Valene! Don't you know what an Avalanche is?" Jeff asked mockingly. "They show them on TV all the time."

"I'm afraid I don't keep up on things like that," she confessed, with a sideways glance toward Jordan.

He let out a chuckle as he caught Jeff's face in the rearview mirror. "Women don't care as much about that sorta stuff as us guys, Jeff."

"I know it's the nicest truck I've ever been in," Valene admitted. "I love the leathery smell. It must be quite new."

"As a matter of fact, I've only had it for two months now, so I guess you could say it's pretty new."

"I want an Avalanche when I grow up," Jeff said.

Jordan let loose a little laugh. "Jeff, by the time you get

ready to buy a truck, they'll probably have wings!"

"Really?"

"He's teasing you, Jeff," Valene said, smiling over the seat at her nephew.

"Hey, Valene," Jordan inserted. "Did you give any more thought to my plan? About caring for Hero when he comes home tomorrow?"

"Yes, but I still think it's asking too much of you."

"It's not. Honest. I think it's the best thing we could come up with. I say, let's do it!"

❧

Hero was wide awake and struggling against the straps that restrained him when they entered the cubicle. His fur was damp.

"Don't be alarmed," Dr. Bainbridge said as he began to unfasten Hero's straps. "He had his water therapy session, and you know how Labs love water."

Jordan moved to the dog's side and placed a hand on his damp fur. "Does that kind of therapy really help him?"

"Oh, yes. You'll want to continue his water therapy when you get him home," Dr. Bainbridge explained. "Simply fill the tub about half full and lower him into it. It'll not only make him feel better, but the water will give him some buoyancy and make it easier for him to stand. Just make sure you have an abundance of old towels. He splashes quite a bit."

Jordan flashed a quick look toward Valene. "I don't think you'll want to try this without me."

She nodded. "You're right. I could never handle him by myself."

"There's something else I need to mention." The doctor handed one end of the towel to Valene. "Hero will be standing by himself in a couple of weeks, he'll be able to walk very soon after that, and then run, but he'll always appear a bit stiff when he walks. Those hips are never going to be quite right, and he may develop arthritis in them sooner than normal. I just want you to be aware of it, so you'll recognize it when it comes."

"I've heard arthritis is fairly common in older Labradors, Doc. Is that true?"

"Yes, it's common in many older dogs, but Hero is young, and he should have many good years ahead of him." He ruffled up the dog's damp fur. "As you can see, his abrasions are healing nicely, and his fur is beginning to grow back, but you'll still have to keep those places quite clean and continue to give him his amoxicillin for awhile. I've already taken the stitches out of those cuts he had." He pointed to several places on Hero's shoulders. "I'll have all the instructions written out for you when you come for him tomorrow. He'll also need to continue with the Rimadyl twice a day. In some ways, this is going to require more effort on your part than taking a new baby home from the hospital, only thing is, you won't have to burp him."

Jordan laughed. "Gonna be a few years before that happens!"

His comment only reinforced Valene's resolve to keep their relationship from going beyond friendship, though she'd like see it go much farther.

"He still looks sorta funny," Jeff said, wrinkling up his nose.

"He'll look fine, once that fur grows back," the doctor assured him. "Just be patient."

They worked with Hero, helping him drag his body by using the towel, until he seemed exhausted.

"I think he's had enough for one day." Dr. Bainbridge pulled the towel from beneath the dog. "I'll give him his dose of Rimadyl, and he'll soon be fast asleep."

"He looks so pitiful," Valene whispered to Jordan as the doctor left them alone. "Will he ever be himself again?"

Jordan took her hand in his and stroked her knuckles with the pad of his thumb. "Of course, he'll be alright. He has the two of us to help him."

"I'm so thankful for you," she declared as they stood by the dog's side. "I couldn't have faced this without you."

"If I hadn't been around, Hero might not be here now," he said with a sorrowful expression.

She shrugged. "But what happened, happened, and you've been with me right from the start. I really do appreciate all the things you've done for both Hero and me."

"Enough! I don't deserve this kind of praise."

They stayed until Hero was resting comfortably. Valene bent over Hero and whispered her love and good wishes for his returning health, adding that she was praying for him and his recovery, before she kissed the tip of his ear and said good-bye. Then Jordan ushered her and Jeff out the door and to his truck.

"How about spaghetti and meatballs for supper, Jeff?" Jordan asked as he turned the key in the ignition. "I know a great place right on the way back to the condo."

"Um, I like spaghetti," Jeff answered quickly, leaning over the back of the front seat.

"You shouldn't, Jordan," Valene said, shaking her head. "You really don't have to feed us every night. And remember, I was going to cook tonight."

"Have to? Did anyone here twist my arm?" he asked with a grin, keeping his eyes trained on the road. "Besides, I like taking you out to eat."

"I can fix us something when we get home," she volunteered, afraid they were taking advantage of his generosity.

"I really want to take you and Jeff. Please say yes."

What could she say? He wanted to take them, and Jeff wanted to go. "Okay, but this has got to end. Tomorrow night, I definitely will cook."

"Does that mean you're inviting me to supper?"

She laughed. "Of course, you're invited, but don't expect anything fancy. I'm not much of a cook, but I'm learning."

Before they arrived at the condo, Jordan's cell phone rang. From what Valene could hear of the one-sided conversation, it was one of his navy buddies. His car wouldn't start, and he wanted Jordan to bring over his jumper cables.

He looked disappointed as he explained and placed the phone on his belt. "I'll have to give you a rain check on the spaghetti, and you two are going to have to play Clue without me."

"We were going to play Clue?" Jeff asked from the backseat. "Yippee!"

Valene swatted at Jordan's arm playfully. "Looks like you got out of that one easily enough. But now I'm going to have to play, thanks to you."

"I'll make it up to you," he said, grinning at her. "Since someone is covering for me tomorrow, I can go with you to pick up Hero anytime you're ready," he told her as she stood on the sidewalk, with Jeff at her side.

"Why don't we plan on going about ten? That okay?"

"Ten, it is."

She watched as the truck pulled out of the parking lot and onto the street.

"You ought to marry him, Aunt Val. He's nice."

She gave her nephew a sad look. "He's not the marrying kind, Jeff. He has plans to see the world before he settles down. That could be years from now."

"Maybe you could see the world with him."

Oh, if only it were that simple. "I don't think the navy would let a wife tag along."

"So, pray about it!"

Out of the mouths of babes. "You're one smart kid," Valene

told her nephew as she put an arm about him and they headed for their front door. "I will pray about it."

⛝

Jordan pulled into his buddy's driveway and stopped opposite his car.

"Hope I didn't take you away from something important," his friend said as Jordan opened the cargo bay and pulled out the jumper cables.

"Naw, I was just in the company of a beautiful woman, that's all."

"What'd you do with her? I don't see her in the truck."

"I told her duty calls and dropped her off at her place."

"Sounds like I spoiled your evening. Why didn't you tell me? Maybe I could've gotten hold of someone else."

Jordan grinned as he snapped the jumper cable clamps over the battery's terminals. "Yeah, I had a terrific evening planned. I was gonna play Clue with her six-year-old nephew. Look what you made me miss."

"I hate that game! My daughter wants me to play it with her all the time. If I ever meet Colonel Mustard, I'm gonna strangle him myself! The guy who invented that game must not have had kids!" His buddy shook his head. "No man in his right man would put himself through that kind of torture unless he was bonkers about the woman. When's the wedding?"

Jordan offered a feeble laugh. Somehow the single life didn't seem as satisfying as it used to, but he'd never admit it to his buddies. "No wedding! I'm gonna see the world before I get saddled down with a wife, remember?"

The man gave him a friendly slap on his back. "You sure about that? Seems to me you've met a woman who might just change your mind."

"Nope. Just a friend."

Jordan checked the connections one more time, then

motioned for the man to turn on the ignition. The car's engine roared into action. He disconnected the cables and began rolling them up.

"Hey, thanks, Jordan. I really appreciate your help. Guess I'd better buy that new battery tomorrow."

"No problem. That's what friends are for. You'd have done the same thing for me."

The man smiled. "I'm not so sure I'd have left a beautiful woman to come to your aid. If you hurry, you might get back in time to play that game of Clue."

Jordan climbed into his pickup, rolled down the window, and gave the man a wave. "I'll give your regards to Colonel Mustard!"

The light was on in Valene's condo when he drove by, and he was tempted to stop. But tomorrow was a big day for her. Hero was coming home.

&

"Jeff's fine. He didn't even get a scratch," Valene told her twin as they talked on the telephone. "He didn't mean to disobey, honest. I'd told him to stay on the sidewalk, but you know how the sidewalks all end at the parking lot here in our complex. Jeff got to the end and couldn't stop. Jordan was driving fairly slow and slammed on his brakes in time to avoid hitting him. Hero wasn't that fortunate."

"I just feel awful about this," Vanessa said on the other end. "I praise God Jeff is alright, but I know how much you love that dog. Jordan—is that the man's name who hit Hero?"

"Yes, he's been wonderful to us. And Hero's going to be alright. It'll take time, but with Jordan's help. . ."

"He's going to help you with Hero?"

"Oh, Vanessa, I can't wait for you to meet him. He's the most amazing man. He's paying all of the vet bills, and he's going to help me with Hero's exercises and water therapy.

He's been driving me to the vet's every—"

"Whoa, Sis! Who is this man? He sounds like saint! Why do I get the feeling you're interested in him? Do I detect a bit of infatuation here?"

"No!"

"You could've fooled me. How old is this man anyway?"

Valene twisted the phone cord about her finger nervously. "I'm not really sure. Several years older than us, I guess. Maybe even thirty. We've never talked about age."

"He lives near you?"

"Yes, he has a condo a few doors down, but he's a navy pilot. Sometimes he stays on the San Diego base."

"I can hardly wait to meet him. But Val, if you want him, you should go after him. I've never heard you talk about a man with such enthusiasm. He is a Christian, isn't he?"

"Yes, praise God, he is. But I could never go after him. I'm not like you. Besides, he's made it perfectly clear he's going to see the world before he settles down. That could be years from now."

"You wouldn't be the first woman to change a man's mind."

"Since he's a Christian, I might be tempted to try, but there's no way he'd be interested in me."

"Why? You're gorgeous!"

Val chuckled. "You're only saying that because we look exactly alike!"

"Val, you always cut yourself down," Vanessa protested. "I can't imagine any man not being attracted to you."

"So, how's the honeymoon going?" Valene asked, needing to change the subject before she confessed how fond she was growing of Jordan. She'd never been able to keep a secret from her sister for very long. "Is Nathan as wonderful as you thought, now that you're with him twenty-four/seven?"

"He's even more wonderful. Oh, Val, Ireland is beautiful.

Better than anything I could imagine! We're having a terrific time, but I know Nathan is anxious to get back to Jeff. Are Mom and Dad still coming after Jeff on Saturday?"

"That's the plan. But I've thoroughly enjoyed having Jeff here. I'm afraid it's been pretty boring for him though, with all the trips to the vet's. He's stayed with Diane a couple of times. He and her son always have a great time together."

"I know they do. Jeff's told me, and I like Diane. Well, I'd better let you go before my dear husband pulls the phone from my hand and hangs it up. I know he'll feel better about Jeff's near-accident now that I've talked to you. I hope all this hasn't been too trying for you."

"I'll survive. Just enjoy your honeymoon."

Valene stared into the phone. *Why can't I be more like Vanessa? When she finally decided she wanted Nathan she went after him. Not me. I'll sit on the sidelines and let Jordan slip through my fingers. As if he'd ever be interested in the likes of me!*

❧

Jeff chattered about everything from Clue to his new Rollerblades, to bicycling, to frogs, as the three rode along on their way to the animal clinic the next morning.

"I'm nervous," Valene finally got in edgewise between Jeff's words about a cartoon he'd seen.

Jordan gave her a frown. "Why? The doc said he'd be ready to come home today."

"It's so hard to see him in pain. I'm afraid I'll hurt him."

Without looking away from the road, he reached over, took her hand, and gave it a squeeze. "You're not going to hurt him. Besides, I'll be there to help you. You'll do fine. That dog loves you. He knows you wouldn't hurt him intentionally."

"Oh, Jordan, what would I do without you?"

He gave her a grin. "Funny you should ask. I was wondering what I was going to do without you when this is all over. You kinda grow on a guy."

"Like fungus?"

"No, Silly. You know what I mean."

"What's fungus?" a small voice asked from the backseat.

Valene let out a giggle. "It's a weird-looking kind of stuff that grows on trees."

"All fuzzy and green and nasty," Jordan added, screwing up his face.

Valene turned her head away. "Yuck! Did you have to say that?"

"You're the one who brought up the word fungus. Not me!"

"I guess I did."

"Hey, my words were only meant in the kindest way," Jordan explained with a grin as his fingers tightened over hers. "A compliment. Not my fault if you made light of them."

Valene sat still, not knowing if she should squeeze his hand back or just ignore it. "In that case, I thank you."

"You and Jeff go on back and see Hero," Jordan told them as they entered the clinic. "I need to take care of the bill."

Valene shook her head. "I can't let you pay for all of it, Jordan. That's asking too much. He is my dog."

He tapped the little bell on the counter to signal the receptionist they were there. "Look, I said I was going to pay Hero's bill, and I meant it. It's important to me that I do."

The woman appeared with the dog's long, itemized bill and handed it to Jordan. Valene gasped when she saw the total. It was far more than she'd anticipated, but he barely seemed to notice as he signed the charge slip.

She grabbed onto his arm. "Oh, Jordan. I had no idea it would be so much!"

"Don't worry about it."

"But I do worry about it."

He bent and kissed her cheek. "Best money I ever spent."

ॐ

Hero was lying on his side, fresh from a bath and his water therapy. The doctor's assistant was drying him off with a hair dryer.

"Well, don't you look handsome," Valene told the dog as she rushed to his side. "And you smell good too!"

Hero lifted his head a bit, the whites of his eyes showing as he gave a slight whimper.

"We've come to take you home, Hero," Valene said sweetly as she stroked her friend. She scooted to one side and made room for Jeff.

"Hi, Boy," Jeff said, patting the dog's damp back. "Sorry you got hurt chasing me."

Dr. Bainbridge came in, carrying two bottles of pills and a sheet filled with instructions. He conferred with the two of them, covering each point in great detail. "Any questions?" he asked finally.

Jordan shook his head. "None that come to mind right now. How about you, Valene?"

She took her attention away from Hero. "I noticed you have him lying on what looks like shredded newspaper. Should we do that too?"

The doctor gave a slight snicker. "It'd sure make it easier to clean up after him until he can get on his feet and go outside. If you're planning on keeping him in the house, I'd recommend using a large piece of cardboard or a crate of some kind for his bed, then cover it with a piece of plastic and a thick layer of the shredded paper."

"I've already got a big bag of shredded paper in my computer room, and I can get as much as we'll need from the base," Jordan told her. "And I always keep a large piece of cardboard on the bed of my truck. I'll bring it in for him."

"Well, you've taken care of his bill. It looks like he's

ready to go home." Dr. Bainbridge turned toward Jordan after handing the bag containing Hero's medication to Valene. "I'd like to shake your hand, young man. In all my years as a veterinarian, I've never seen anyone face up to his responsibilities any more than you have."

Valene smiled. "He's been a rock through this whole ordeal."

"Okay, you two. Enough. I've only done what's right. Now," Jordan said moving toward Hero, "let's take this guy home." He carefully slipped his arms beneath the dog and gently lifted his rigid body, cradling him against his chest.

When they reached the pickup, Jordan held Hero while Valene unlocked the cab, removed an old army blanket from the truck's cargo area, and spread it across the backseat.

"Valene, why don't you ride back there with Hero, and Jeff can ride up front with me? I think Hero would be much calmer with you sitting next to him."

She smiled to herself as she climbed in beside the big dog. Every inch of Jordan's Avalanche was spotlessly clean and highly polished. Not one speck of dust anywhere, not even in the cargo area. But here he was, insisting Hero ride on the leather seat instead of in the truck bed. What a man!

Once everyone was in their place and Hero seemed settled, Jordan turned the key in the ignition. "Hang on, Hero. We're taking you home."

๖

Jeff held his nose and backed away quickly. "Aunt Valene, come quick. Hero smells!"

"It's okay, Jeff. He can't help himself." She rushed to the makeshift bed on the floor of her living room and dropped to her knees. "Wet one of these big rags, then get me one of those large paper grocery sacks from under the sink."

"Let me clean him up." Jordan dropped to his knees beside her and tried to push her away, but she held her ground.

"Absolutely not. You've already done too much."

"Valene, you shouldn't be lifting him. He's too heavy, and you'll have to put clean paper under him. Let me at least lift him for you."

She sent him a grateful smile. "Thanks. That would help."

Although Hero let out a yelp when Jordan lifted him, he quickly settled down. It took less than five minutes to get him cleaned up and back into a comfortable position on a fresh layer of shredded paper.

"Poor thing. I know he's in pain," Valene said, leaning over Hero and stroking his back.

"Hopefully that Rimadyl the doc gave him this morning is at least taking the edge off."

"Can't you give him an aspirin?" Jeff asked.

"Rimadyl is sorta like an aspirin, Sweetie, only for dogs," Valene explained. "I know you're bored. Why don't you go into my bedroom and watch that new adventure videotape I got for you?"

"Okay!"

"Good idea," Jordan said. "There for a minute I was afraid you were going to suggest we all play Clue." He patted the sofa cushion beside him. "Come and sit with me. You don't have to stay by Hero every minute."

She gave one last pat to the dog's back, then moved to sit by Jordan. "I hadn't realized how heavy Hero'd gotten. I never could've gotten him home without you."

"Sure you could. All it would've taken was one call to one of your old boyfriends, and I'll bet he'd come running."

She wished that were so. But unfortunately, her old boyfriends were few and far between. Unlike her sister, she'd never been an active part of the college dating scene. Not that Vanessa hadn't tried to set her up. She had. But the kind of flamboyant, hunky guys that seemed to be drawn to her sister were not Val's cup of tea. Most of those dates had been a major disaster, for both her and the man. She was sure she'd been a complete bore. Witty remarks and over-the-top conversation had never come easy to her. Rarely had there been a second date. To her, it seemed a waste of time to spend an evening with some jock who thought burping was a talent, no matter how popular he was.

Before she could explain, Jordan's cell phone rang.

"Hi." He turned to Valene and mouthed the word Mom. "No, I can't. Not this weekend. But I'll come and see you and Dad soon. I promise."

Valene picked up a magazine from the table and leafed through it, feeling very awkward listening to his side of the conversation.

"I'll call when I know, Mom. Tell Dad hello for me." He grinned as he placed the phone back onto his belt. "She still tries to run my life. Your mom do that to you?"

"Some. She doesn't like the idea of me living here in Spring Valley. I have to keep reminding her I'm only fifteen miles away, and I do see them at church every Sunday. How did your parents feel about you joining the navy?"

"Oh, that was no problem. My dad graduated from the Naval Academy in Annapolis and served out his time before he joined my grandfather in our family business. Dad loved seeing the world before he settled down and got married. And he loved the navy. From the time I was a little boy, my life has been planned out for me. I studied hard, made good grades, and like my dad, got an appointment to Annapolis. Only instead of serving on a ship as part of the onboard crew like my father did, I opted for flying an F-18 and landing on one. Most guys know that sweet little number as the Hornet.

It's the perfect plane for taking off and landing on an aircraft carrier."

"It sounds scary. Aren't you ever afraid you'll miss?"

"Naw, you get used to it. Like anything else you do in the navy, you train for it. It's second nature now." He gave her a mischievous smile. "I could almost take off and land with my eyes closed."

She winced. "Please promise me you won't even try."

He became serious. "I'm only kidding. When I'm flying that F-18, I'm all business. Every split second counts and could mean life or death."

"Life is very fragile. I'm glad to hear you're being careful." *And I'm thankful God is your copilot.*

"I've just about completed my obligatory time as a navy pilot, but I plan to stay in another four years or so, then join my father in the business."

"I guess you love flying."

"It gets into your blood. I like the navy too, and I've seen quite a bit of the world, but not as much as I'd like."

"Do you ever worry about having to fly into dangerous areas? There always seems to be so much turmoil."

He paused thoughtfully. "Sometimes, but it's my duty to go where I'm needed. I not only love flying, I enjoy visiting other countries and learning about their cultures, but there's no place like the good old USA. I'm willing to do whatever it takes to protect her."

"Have you ever been in danger?"

His face sobered. "A number of times. Danger goes with the territory. I've been lucky. Some of my friends haven't. But I'd rather not talk about it."

"I'm sorry. I didn't mean to pry."

He slipped an arm about her shoulders and drew her close to him. "You're not prying. It's just that I'd prefer to forget those episodes. I made it through. That's what counts."

"When you were in danger. . ." She stopped mid-sentence, not exactly sure how she should finish.

"Yes?"

"Did you. . .pray?"

He stared off in space a bit. "Yeah, I prayed. Sometimes I wasn't sure God heard me, but I made it out alive. I've always wondered what would've happened to me if I hadn't prayed. Guess I'll never know."

"I don't know how people get through life without praying," she added timidly.

"Like when you prayed for Hero? Boy, I thought sure he was a goner. He was so still when I picked him up off that parking lot."

She sent a loving glance toward the sleeping dog. "I knew if he was to survive, God would have to perform a miracle."

"Well, if your prayers were what kept him alive, I'm grateful you prayed and God answered your prayer. I couldn't have lived with myself if Hero'd died, knowing how much he means to you."

Valene placed her hand on his sleeve. "We can't understand why things like this happen, but I know God wants only the best for me."

"Are you saying Hero's long, difficult recovery is best for you? For the next few weeks, your whole life is going to revolve around caring for that dog. Where is the good in that?"

She gave him a shy grin. "I—I met you."

He frowned. "That's the good? Meeting me? How can you say that?"

"You asked me about my old boyfriends." She paused and forced back the tears she was afraid would rise to the surface. "I've never told this to anyone, except my mom. I'm not even sure I should tell you."

"You can tell me anything, Valene. I'm here for you." His tone was kind, and for some unknown reason, she knew he'd never betray her confidence.

She took a deep breath and began. "My last year in college, one of the stars on the swim team asked me out to dinner. He was extremely popular, and I was flattered. I didn't even tell Vanessa about his invitation. She'd gone to some seminar that weekend about training guide dogs. I borrowed one of my sister's dresses from her closet and even fixed my hair like hers, hoping I'd be appear more attractive than my plain old, dull self."

"I haven't seen your sister, but I can't imagine anyone being more attractive than you."

She gave him an appreciative smile. "We had a wonderful dinner at a quaint little restaurant out in the country. I laughed and tried to be witty and charming, like I'd seen Vanessa do. We talked and talked, and I was actually beginning to think he liked me." She gulped hard at the lump rising in her throat, just remembering that evening.

"When he turned off the highway and into an industrial area, I questioned him about it. He explained he was taking a shortcut back to town. Gullible me, I believed him."

Jordan winced. "I think I know where this story is going."

"Yes, it's the same old story we've heard time and again, but I was foolish enough to believe it couldn't happen to me."

"A wrestling match, huh?"

She lowered her eyes and bit at her lip. "Yes."

His grip tightened about her shoulders, and he pulled her close. "I'm so sorry. Guys like that give us all a bad name."

"I panicked. I didn't know what to do. In desperation, I grabbed the door handle and jumped out of his car when he stopped at a stop sign."

"Did—did he follow you?"

"No, he didn't. Although I was terrified, I knew I wasn't alone. I felt God's presence. The man made a terrible obscene remark I won't repeat and drove off, leaving me there. When I finally found a phone, I called my mom to come and pick me up. I've never been so scared."

"Whew! I was so afraid he'd—"

"But he didn't, Jordan. Since then, I've pretty much avoided all men. Up to that time, I'd heard nothing but good things about that guy. Just shows how you never really know someone."

"I'm not that way, Valene. I hope you know that."

She smiled up at him. "I do know that, Jordan. You've restored my faith in men. That's what I meant when I said something good came out of all of this."

"Hey, don't let your guard down because of me. I couldn't stand the idea of anything happening to you. I'm in the navy, remember? I hear how some guys talk, and it makes me sick."

"I can imagine. I do believe God sent you to me though. To show me there are fine men in this world. If only—"

"If only what?"

"Never mind."

"No, I want to know what you were going to say. If only what?"

"If—if only I could find a good man. . .like you." There, she'd said it.

He grimaced, then smiled. "I do try to be a good man. I don't cheat on my income taxes. I help old ladies across the street."

The look on Jordan's face confused her. It was as though he were a million miles away, remembering a painful time in his life. She wanted to ask him about it. Hadn't she just shared her innermost secret with him? But somehow, she couldn't. She just couldn't.

"There are some things even God can't forgive," he said slowly, enunciating every word.

She planted a hand on her hip. "That's not true, Jordan. God is able to forgive anything and everything, but we have to ask Him. The only thing He can't forgive is if we turn our back on Him and reject Him."

"I wish I could believe that."

"You can." *God, give me the right words, please.* "I can show you in God's Word where He talks about forgiveness. You're such a kind man, Jordan. It's hard to imagine you ever doing anything bad enough to make you feel God couldn't forgive you for it."

He stood quickly, brushing his hands together. "Let's talk about more pleasant things. What do you want for supper?"

&

After a hastily prepared supper, Jordan helped Valene clear the table and put the dishes in the dishwasher. He'd done the same thing hundreds of times in his own condo and had always thought of it as work. But tonight, doing it with Valene, it was fun. He actually found himself enjoying the task.

"You look cute in that apron," she told him with a giggle as she pressed the dishwasher's on button. "I wish I had new batteries in my digital camera. I'd take your picture."

"So you could blackmail me? No, thanks." He untied the apron and placed it back on the hook. "I put clean sheets on my bed, and I made up a bed on my sofa for Jeff. You ought to try to get to bed early. You've had a pretty busy day. Hero will be fine with me. He's had his Rimadyl and should sleep pretty well for the next few hours."

"I'm not going to run you out of your bed. You've had a busy day too."

He pulled his keys from his pocket and handed them to her. "Valene, I hate to be tough about this, but we've already discussed this once. I'm going to spend the nights on your sofa so I can take care of Hero. You and Jeff go on over to my condo. Everything is ready for you, and I refuse to take no for an answer."

Jeff grabbed his aunt's hand. "We're gonna sleep in Jordan's condo? Kewl!"

"No, Jeff. We—"

"Valene, I mean it. I am going to stay here nights and take care of Hero. Once he begins to get on his feet, we'll reevaluate the sleeping arrangements. But until then, I'm staying here. Don't even think about arguing with me."

"But—"

He held up his palm between them. "No buts. Now get whatever you'll need, and go."

Jeff tugged on her hand. "Come on, Aunt Valene. It'll be fun."

"Well, if you're sure. . ."

"I am sure. Now go. I'll be over in the morning about six. I need to be on the base by seven."

"I need to change the sheets first, and—"

"Go!" he said firmly. "I'm not afraid of your germs. Besides, I can sleep on the couch."

"If you're going to sleep on the couch, then I'm not going," she said, resolutely crossing her arms.

He held up both palms in surrender. "Okay. I'll sleep in the bed."

Once the door had closed behind Valene and Jeff, Jordan wandered into the kitchen and had a cup of the coffee she'd put on to brew before she left. He checked Hero, then settled himself onto the sofa and clicked the TV remote. He flipped from channel to channel, finding nothing that interested him, and was ready to forget it and hit the off button when he heard music. He paused, turned up the volume, and began to listen, snapping his fingers to the beat.

The singer was extolling God's grace and His forgiveness. He started to turn it off or switch to another channel but felt compelled to listen. When the song ended, he turned the TV off.

He picked up the little case he'd brought with him and moved into Valene's bathroom to prepare for bed. There, taped to the mirror, was a verse that he knew had to be from the Bible. She'd told him she regularly memorized Scripture. Maybe this was how she did it. He leaned toward it and read aloud, "If we confess our sins, He is faithful and just to forgive us our sins, and to cleanse us from all unrighteousness. If we say that we have not sinned, we make Him a liar, and His word is not in us." The words went right to his heart. *Oh, Valene, you have no idea how I've sinned.*

Had she taped that on her mirror, knowing he'd see it? Of course not! Hadn't she tried to talk him out of staying in her condo for the night? He showered, slipped into his T-shirt and boxers, gathered up his things, and after checking on Hero, headed for Valene's bed. He set his alarm clock, pulled back the covers, and crawled in, taking note of the sweet-smelling scent on the pillow. The bed felt good.

Before he reached for the light switch on the bedside lamp, he glanced at his new surroundings. It looked like Valene, with soft, feminine ruffles and frills everywhere in the room. A huge white teddy bear sat in a white wicker rocker opposite the bed, smiling at him. He smiled back. A pile of Christian romance novels stood in a neat stack on the nightstand, flanked by an assortment of hand and body creams. He lifted the lid on the one marked honeysuckle and took in a deep whiff. He'd noticed the fragrance on Valene that very day.

Visions of the lovely woman, no doubt sleeping in his bed by now, filled his mind. He'd never met anyone like her. If he could've laid out a recipe for the type of woman he'd like to marry eventually, it would describe Valene. Shy, unassuming, loving Valene. Her story about the college jock really disturbed him. Guys like that belonged in jail. Unfortunately, innocent women like Valene were entirely too trustful for their own good.

He glanced at the lace curtains covering the windows, the small ceramic birds on a wicker shelf hanging on the wall, and the silver comb-and-brush set on her dresser. He'd never spent a night in a woman's bedroom before. This was a whole new experience, one he was enjoying. With one last stretch, he turned out the light, slipped down between the sheets, and pulled the comfy quilt up over him. Being with Valene these past few days, hearing her laughter, watching her cry, seeing her loving ways with both Jeff and Hero had made him question his determination to see the world before he settled down.

Forget it, Fella, he told himself as he lay there in the darkness surrounded by things that reminded him of her. *Think about your buddies who said the same thing you did. They wanted to see the world too, but when some pretty young thing came along and swept them off their feet, they traded their freedom and independence for a wedding ring and a baby carriage. Not me. I've got a plan for my life, and nothing, not even a woman as beautiful and caring as Valene Zobel, is going to change that plan.*

A whimper, then a moan followed by a yelp brought him quickly to his feet. Hero!

He flipped on the hall light and hurried into the living room. "What's wrong, Boy? Can't you sleep?" Jordan bent over the dog. "Oh, Hero! You smell! Not again!"

❧

Valene glanced at the clock on Jordan's nightstand. Two o'clock. Why was she having so much trouble falling asleep?

Could it be that she was sleeping in Jordan's bed? The scent of his aftershave wafting around her? Or was she worried about Hero?

That's dumb! she told herself as she flipped over onto her back. *Hero is in better hands with Jordan caring for him, than if I was there.* In the shaft of moonlight arching its way across the room, she could see some sort of certificates hanging on the wall. Curiosity getting the better of her, she crawled out of bed, turned on the light, and padded her way across the room. They were awards of some kind. She gasped as she read the various inscriptions. Every one of them was an award for bravery. Jordan was a hero? Were these for the incidents he'd mentioned but was unwilling to talk about when she'd asked him if he'd ever been in danger? She'd like to know more, but considering how adamant he'd been about not discussing it, she decided to keep her questions to herself. For now, at least.

She turned out the light and moved to the window. From his bedroom, she could barely see one of her windows through the bushes and trees that surrounded the complex. Was Jordan getting any sleep, or was Hero keeping him awake? She should've stayed with Hero herself. Jordan needed his sleep too. Especially since he seemed to have so many obligations at the base. Why had she ever let him talk her into such a ridiculous arrangement?

Finally, she crawled back into bed. As she lay on his pillow and stared at the ceiling, she couldn't help but wonder what it would be like to be married to Jordan Young. Eventually, she drifted off to sleep with visions of the handsome pilot filling her dreams.

The ringing of the doorbell brought her out of a sound sleep, and for a moment, she couldn't even think where she was. She grabbed her bathrobe, rushed to the door, peered out the peephole, and, seeing Jordan standing there, pulled open the door a crack. "What are you doing here? Is something wrong with Hero?"

six

"It's six A.M. I'm ready to leave for the base. I was supposed to wake you up, remember?"

She rubbed at her eyes, suddenly realizing she was standing in the doorway in her bathrobe and pajamas. "I'll be right back."

She closed the door, leaving him standing outside his own condo. After rushing into the bedroom and pulling on jeans and a T-shirt, she hurried back to open the door. "Sorry."

He gave her a teasing grin. "I understand."

"Did you get any sleep at all?"

A smiled crooked at his lips. "Hero and I were up a few times during the night, but he settled down about four. After that, I slept so soundly I couldn't even think where I was when my alarm went off."

She dipped her head slightly. "Th–that's the way I felt when you rang the doorbell. Did Hero give you much trouble?"

"Umm, not exactly a lot of trouble, but you'll find some pretty smelly rags in your trash. You might want to dump them right away. I kinda think his medication might be the cause of some of his, um, accidents."

"You may be right. I should've been there," she said, feeling guilty as she crossed her arms to get warmer in the cool, morning air.

"Oh? And you could have lifted him all by yourself?"

"Maybe, but I might've hurt Hero in the process."

"Don't try to lift him while I'm gone. Let Jeff help you. Understand?"

She gave him a mock salute. "Yes, Sir. Give me five minutes to gather my things and wake Jeff up."

He put a hand on her wrist. "No. Leave your things here. You'll be spending the night again."

"Jordan, I can't let you—"

He gave her a playful frown. "Let me? It's my decision. Now scoot! I have to get to the base."

By the time she'd brushed her teeth and raked a comb through her hair, Jordan had awakened Jeff, and the two of them were waiting for her on the porch. Jordan handed Jeff her keys and told him to go open the door. "I'll be back by four," he said to Valene. "And don't try to give Hero his water therapy until I'm here to help you. Do you hear me?"

"Jordan, I can—"

He slipped an arm about her and pulled her close. "I know you can take care of Hero without me, but I want to help. I like being around both of you." He slipped a finger beneath her chin and lifted her face to meet his.

Her heart pounded. It was exactly like her dream.

"You're a very special woman, Valene," he said softly as his lips met hers. "See you at four."

She stood frozen to the spot as she watched him stride across the parking lot to his truck. Jordan Young had kissed her—not on the cheek as he'd done before, but fully on her lips. Could that be why she had goose bumps on her arms? *Oh, God, help me! I already love this man.*

❧

Friday was nearly the same as Thursday, but Hero seemed a bit stronger and even more determined to stand. By Saturday morning, both Valene and Jordan had fallen into an unquestioned routine of spending their nights at the other's condo, and it was working out well.

"Jeff, pack up your things," Valene told her nephew.

"Grandma and Grandpa and Lick will be here soon."

Jeff pulled himself away from the Saturday morning cartoons with a frown. "Aw, Aunt Val, do I have to go? I miss Lick and I wanna see him, but I wanna stay here with you and Hero too."

Her brows lifted in surprise. "You do? I figured you'd been bored staying here. Hero has taken so much of my time, we really haven't been able to do any of the things I'd planned."

"You guys are the only ones who'll play Clue with me," the boy said, his lower lip hanging down. "My dad hates that game, and I like being here with Hero. He's a nice dog."

Valene shot a quick glance at Jordan, who only shrugged. "We haven't really played Clue with you that much," she confessed, wishing they'd played it more often.

Jeff hung his head dejectedly. "I know, but you had Hero to take care of, and I'm the one who got him hurt."

Jordan reached out and pulled the boy onto his lap. "You aren't responsible for what happened, Jeff. Yes, you disobeyed your aunt by riding into the parking lot, but the way that sidewalk ended so abruptly, there was nothing you could do to get stopped in time. I'm just thankful I didn't hit you."

"But I made you hit Hero."

"I should've had him on a leash," Valene inserted.

"No one made me hit Hero. It just happened, and he's going to get well. Now, you just forget about all of this, mind your aunt, and gather up your things."

"You have a way with kids," Valene told him after Jeff disappeared into the bedroom. "You're going to make a great dad someday."

"I'm not so sure. By the time I finish serving my stint with the navy and find me a wife, I may be too old to be the kind of dad I'd like to be."

His words weren't exactly what she wanted to hear, but she

knew anything else would have been wishful thinking on her part. "You won't be that old."

He seemed to be giving her comment some serious thought. "I hope not. My folks had me late in life. My dad never played games with me or attended any of my school functions. He never even made it to my game when I played in the state basketball finals. I want something better for my children."

She gulped. "Children? As in, more than one?"

"Sure. I'd like to have at least four or five."

Jeff came dragging his suitcase into the room, hugging a basketball with his free arm. "Mr. Young, could you shoot some baskets with me while I'm waiting for Grandpa?"

Jordan grinned. "Sure, Sport, if Valene says it's okay."

She nodded, wishing she could leave Hero long enough to go watch them. Maybe even shoot a few baskets herself, although she wasn't very good at it. She left the front door standing open, tidied up the room, put on a fresh pot of coffee, then squatted down beside Hero. Although his hips were stiff and he still couldn't move around much, his tail wagged rapidly. "You're a good boy," she told him as she stroked his ragged fur. "Even with all those funny-looking patches where your fur was worn off, you're still my beautiful dog."

"Yoo hoo! Valene!"

"Come on in, Mom," she answered, pressing one hand against Hero to hold him down.

"Oh, Sweetheart, I can only imagine how hard this has been on you. I know how much you love that dog."

Valene looked past her mother. "Where's Dad?"

"Shooting baskets with his grandson and that gorgeous man out there. Who is that guy?"

"That's Jordan. The man I've been telling you about."

Her mother pulled the footstool up next to Hero's bed and sat down. "You never told me he was that good looking."

"Oh, Mom, he's as nice as he is handsome. I've never met a man like him."

"Is he a Christian, Valene? You know how important that is."

Valene nodded. "Yes, and he's such a good man. You'll like him."

"If you do, I'm sure I will."

Valene patted Hero's back, avoiding her mother's penetrating eyes. "I—I think I'm in love with Jordan."

"Where's my girl?" a man's voice boomed from behind her.

Valene waved a hand in her father's direction. "Here, Daddy, on the floor next to Hero."

He dropped breathlessly onto her sofa, pulled his handkerchief from his pocket, and began wiping his brow. "I'm not as young as I used to be. These guys nearly killed me." He gestured to Jeff and Jordan and Lick who were following close behind.

Valene grinned. "Mom, I'd like you to meet Jordan Young. Jordan, this is my mother, Ellen Zobel."

"Nice to meet you, Mrs. Zobel," Jordan said, wiping his sweaty hand on his knit shirt before extending it. "You have a wonderful daughter."

Her mother flashed a quick look toward Valene as she grabbed onto Lick's collar to settle him down. "I think so, but thanks. I love hearing it from someone else."

Valene felt herself blushing. "Jordan's been a great help with Hero. I don't know what I would've done without him."

Hero let out a yelp as he tried to maneuver himself onto his stomach. As quick as a flash, Jordan rushed to his side, lifting him and holding him so his feet barely touched the floor. "It helps if we change his position pretty often," he explained with a glance toward Valene's parents.

"We've been trying to hold off on giving him his Rimadyl until after he's had his water therapy," Valene added, rising.

"He still looks pretty banged up to me," Mr. Zobel said, bending forward to touch one of Hero's scraped-up areas with his finger. "Will his fur grow back?"

Jordan nodded. "It's already beginning to. He'll never be quite like he was before the accident. The vet say's he'll be able to get around, but his hips'll stay pretty stiff. At least he's alive. That's what matters."

Mr. Zobel put a hand on Jordan's shoulder. "Valene tells us you paid his veterinary bills. That must've set you back a pretty penny."

"I'm the one who hit him, Sir. Paying his bills is the easy part. Nursing him back to health is what's going to take time, but Valene and I are both committed to see it through."

"Which reminds me, Valene. Have you had your phone number changed?" her mother asked.

"No. Why?"

"I tried to phone you a little before six this morning. I knew it was early, but I wanted to ask you about Jeff before Vanessa phoned me. I was sure I dialed the right number, but a man answered. I just hung up and didn't try again."

"Oh, was that you?" Jordan asked quickly.

Mrs. Zobel shot an annoyed glance at Valene, then back to Jordan. "You were in her condo at six this morning?"

"Yes, Ma'am, but I had reason to be here."

"I wasn't here, Mom, because I was asleep over at Jordan's." Valene realized how stupid that sounded after she said it. "So was Jeff."

Her mother frowned and grew quite serious. "I think this calls for an explanation, Valene."

"Look, Mother, Hero needs constant attention. Until he's strong enough to stand. . ." She paused, trying to put Hero's bodily functions into acceptable words. "He has no choice but to, um, mess himself. I can't lift him by myself, so Jordan kindly offered to take the night shift and sleep in my bed."

"While Valene is sleeping over in my condo," Jordan inserted hastily. "Then Valene takes the day shift."

Her father clapped his hands together. "I'd say that's a good, workable plan, wouldn't you, Mother?"

Her mother seemed relieved after things had been explained. "Yes, I guess so. It's very kind of you, Jordan, to help Valene with Hero."

"I stayed at Mr. Young's house too," Jeff said proudly, as if staying there was a real accomplishment. "He plays Clue with me."

"Jeff, did you bring that awful game with you?" his grandmother asked with a slight, teasing frown.

Jeff turned quickly to Jordan. "You like it, don't you, Mr. Young?"

Jordan nodded at the boy. "When I have someone I like to play it with, I do."

"Anything we can do to help you, Honey?" her dad asked.

"Nothing I can think of."

"How about groceries? You need anything?"

She shook her head. "No, Jordan has taken care of that too. I think he nearly bought out the store."

"Well, then, I guess we'll be going." Her father turned to Jeff. "Tell your aunt thanks for taking care of you. Then go put your things in the car, Jeff, and take Lick with you."

Valene slipped an arm about her nephew. "He was a joy to have around. I only wish we could've done more fun things while he was here."

"I had fun!" Jeff said, smiling up at her and hanging onto his dog. "Just being here with you and Hero and Mr. Young was fun."

"I'm glad. Maybe you can come and stay with me another time."

"I'll put your bike in your grandfather's trunk," Jordan told Jeff as the two headed for the door with Lick following. "Just promise me you'll be careful where you ride it, okay?"

Both her father and mother lingered as Jeff and Jordan moved out onto the parking lot.

"You kinda sweet on him?" her father asked, gesturing toward the open door. "I sure hope he's a Christian."

"He is, Dad."

"Valene has always known getting involved with a man who isn't could mean trouble later on," her mother inserted quickly.

"I wasn't exactly Billy Graham when we were dating, Mama." He gave his wife a playful pinch on her arm. "As I recall, your folks weren't too happy about you marrying me. I wasn't a Christian then, or have you forgotten?"

Valene's eyes widened. "You weren't? I always thought you were."

"No, I was about as far from the Lord as a man could get. Oh, I don't mean I was a criminal or anything like that, but I didn't want anything to do with that God stuff. It was only your mother's and her parents' prayers and their godly lives that made me see myself for what I really was. Lost!"

"Daddy, I had no idea! When did you become a Christian?"

Her mother's eyes began to glisten with tears. "When you and your sister were born."

"I nearly lost all three of you, Valene." Her father slipped an arm about her waist. "Having two babies at once is not the same as having one. Your mother had a hard time of it. She spent the last three months of her pregnancy in bed. The night she went into labor, which was about three weeks before her due date, I stood beside her hospital bed feeling totally helpless. Every minute of watching her struggle with you girls' delivery was torture."

He gulped hard before going on. "Finally the doctor turned to me and told me he doubted he'd be able to save all three of you. I—I'll never forget the look in his eyes when he warned me to be prepared for whatever might happen. His final words were, 'Bill, if you know how to pray, pray hard, and pray for a miracle.' I didn't know how I'd ever face life without your mother or be able to raise one or both of you girls by myself. If she died, I wanted to die too."

Valene had never seen her father cry, and she too fought back tears as he dabbed at his eyes with his sleeve, his face more wrinkled with age than she'd ever noticed.

"So many times your mother had explained the plan of salvation to me, but I wouldn't listen. That night her words came back to me, and I could hear them as plain as if she'd just said them. I got down on my knees right there in that delivery room and finally admitted to God I was a sinner. I asked Him to forgive me and accepted Him as my Savior. Then, I promised Him, if He would spare your mother's life and let you girls be born, I'd serve Him until I died. And I meant it. I know now I should never have tried to bargain with God, but I was nothing but a green Christian back then, with very little knowledge of the Scriptures. I'm sure God knew my heart was right, but that's the last time I've tried to bargain with Him."

Valene threw her arms about his neck. "Oh, Daddy. I didn't know. You never told us."

"But, Valene, that doesn't mean a young woman should become involved with a man who doesn't love God the way she does," her mother said, wiping at her own tears. "Sometimes things don't work out for the best."

"Your mother's right," her father said, touching his daughter's arm affectionately. "I'm just sorry it took something that serious to make me see my need for God in my life."

"But Mother, don't you see? Your love for Daddy was what brought him through."

"You have no idea what life was like between your father and me before he accepted the Lord. We were like two corks bobbing in the sea. He went his way. I went mine."

"But God answered your prayers, Mother! How can you not believe the same thing can happen for other women?"

"The bike is in your trunk, and Jeff and Lick are waiting in the car," Jordan said, as he walked through the open door.

"Then we'd better be going," her mother said, with a meaningful glance toward Valene.

"Good-bye, my little sweetie," her father told her as she slipped an arm about his waist and walked him to the door. Then, with a wink, he whispered, "I like your young man. I'll be praying for you. Just don't try to rush things. Wait on the Lord. If He wants you two to get together, He'll make it happen."

Valene and Jordan stood on the porch and waved as her parents' car exited the parking lot.

"Did I come in at a bad time?" Jordan asked once the car was out of sight. "I kinda got the impression your mother wasn't too enthused about me being here with you."

"She only does what all mothers do—worry about their children."

They gave Hero his water therapy, then Valene dried him with her hair dryer as Jordan held him so the dog's feet barely touched the bathroom countertop.

"Do you realize it's been a week since the accident?" he asked as Hero struggled to stand. "I'd say he's making good progress."

"Thanks to you." She smiled up at him.

While Jordan held Hero on his lap, Valene bagged up the soiled shredded paper and replaced it with a fresh batch. Once Hero was settled, Jordan gave him his Rimadyl, followed by his dose of amoxicillin. "I think his skinned-up places look pretty good, don't you?"

Valene leaned over the dog and checked each abrasion carefully. "Doesn't look like any of them have become infected. I think he's well on his way to recovery. As soon as that fur fills in, he'll look as handsome as ever."

She sat down by Jordan, gently stroking Hero's back until he fell asleep.

"I'm not sure your mother likes me," Jordan said.

"Of course, she does. What's not to like? You're a fine man. I know my dad likes you. He told me so."

Jordan brightened. "He did?"

She nodded. "Yes, he did. Right before he left."

"I like him too. You should've seen him shooting baskets. He was pretty good. Probably made at least one out of every four shots. Wish my dad would have shot baskets with me like that."

"I think Mom worries about me because of Vanessa."

"Your sister? What's she got to do with it?"

"Vanessa always knew where she was going and how she was going to get there. I didn't." She gave a feeble laugh. "I still don't."

"I don't understand."

"Vanessa was the feisty one. I spent most of my time trying to keep her out of trouble. Not that she was a bad kid—she wasn't. But she wanted to enjoy life to the fullest. From the time she was a child and we had that little dog, she knew she wanted to work with animals, and she set out a plan to do it. Much like you did with the navy. She got her degree as a veterinary assistant, just like she'd planned. Now she's not only using that degree, she's doing something worthwhile, training service dogs. What am I doing? Working as a medical records assistant at a hospital. I've never once used my degree in marketing, despite the four years I spent in college to earn it. I'm working at a dead-end job for just over minimum wage. We couldn't be more different."

"I think you're selling yourself short, Valene. You're a beautiful, intelligent woman. You shouldn't be comparing yourself to your sister."

She smiled and patted his hand. "Thanks. Your affirmation helps."

"Only telling the truth." He stood and lowered Hero into his bed. "Think you can handle him for a few hours? I need to work on my computer for awhile, then, after I call my parents, I thought I'd grab a quick nap."

"Sure. Go ahead. If I need you, I'll call. I've got a book I want to read."

He grinned. "One of those romance novels I saw on your nightstand? Those looked pretty interesting."

She gave him a coy smile. "Maybe."

She watched as he moved out the door and closed it behind him. There was no use denying it. She was in love with Jordan.

If only he were in love with her.

Although the book was interesting and the characters enthralling, she couldn't keep her mind on the story. She was tired of living vicariously through those characters. It was time she experienced real love firsthand.

She started up her computer and sent off a few E-mails, checked some items on the Internet, then browsed a couple of Christian Web sites. After that, she changed the shredded paper in Hero's bed and stroked his fur, telling him how much she loved him. By three, she was checking the clock every five minutes. All she could think about was the handsome pilot.

At four, a knock sounded on her door.

"Guess what! I ran into Diane on the way over here, and she volunteered to stay with Hero in the morning so you can go to church!"

Val gave Jordan a puzzled look. Hadn't he told her he'd be available all weekend to help her with Hero? "Are you flying tomorrow?"

"No, I thought I'd drive you."

She felt like pinching herself to see if she had fallen asleep and hadn't realized it. "To church?"

"Of course, to church. Don't you want to go?"

She nodded, still not sure she was hearing him right. "Yes, but—"

"I'll go to my own church if you don't you want me to go with you."

"I'd love for you to go with me, but I thought you said—"

"What time should we leave? I have to tell Diane."

"I usually go to the middle service. It starts at nine-thirty. We should leave no later than nine, I guess." His words sent her reeling.

"Good, I'll tell Diane."

She stood in the doorway, feeling numb. *Are you answering my prayers, God? Or am I reading something into this I shouldn't be?*

He came back, carrying a grocery sack. "I told her."

She nodded. "Good. Are you sure she wants to do this?"

"Yep," he said, pushing past her, "Her boy is coming with her. He can help her if Hero has to be lifted. I told her if he made any real messes to just put a heavy layer of fresh paper on it, and I'd clean it up when we got back. And that's not all. She's agreed to come over and stay with Hero during the day when you go back to work next week. Her boy'll be back in school, and she'll be alone all day."

"How much are you paying her, Jordan?"

His grin told her he wasn't about to tell her. "Enough to make it worth her while."

He headed toward the kitchen but stopped long enough to call back over his shoulder, "Steak sound good for supper? I brought over three nice big ribeyes. One for you, one for me, and one for Hero. I'm gonna stick some baking potatoes in the oven, and after I get the grill fired up, I'll put the steaks on to cook."

Valene's jaw dropped. How could one man be so nice? "I'll fix a salad."

❧

Once again, Val spent the night in Jordan's condo, and he in hers. Things were working out quite well. They exchanged condos at eight that morning, in order to give each other time to get ready for church.

Although her mother and father were surprised to see them come in, they welcomed Jordan cordially. Jeff insisted on sitting with them during the service. Valene could feel the eyes of those sitting around her, and she knew they were wondering what a good-looking man like Jordan was doing with her. He sang along with the congregation and was quite attentive during the sermon.

Everyone greeted him in a friendly manner at the close of the service, and he shook hands with all the men, as if he were glad to meet them. He even told the pastor, as he shook his hand on the way out of church, that he'd be back again.

They stopped at a drive-in on the way home and ordered carryout fried chicken dinners, since Valene thought it was only fair they get back and relieve Diane as soon as possible.

Once they were seated around her kitchen table, and she'd prayed over their meal, Jordan dropped a bombshell.

seven

"My parents are having a dinner party next weekend. I want you to come with me."

Valene stared at him. *He wants me to meet his parents?* "I–I thought they lived in La Jolla."

"They do. I thought we'd go for the weekend."

"Oh, Jordan, I don't know. Are you sure you want me to go along? I can probably handle Hero by myself by then. Why don't you go on without me?"

He reached across the table and cupped her hand in his. "I want you to go with me. Please say yes. It'll be fun."

"I–I don't know. I'm not very good at meeting people."

He gave her hand a reassuring squeeze. "You'll do fine. Hey, it's only a dinner party. No big deal. Besides, I want you to see where I grew up. Meet a few of my friends. And we'll take Hero with us. Come on. For me?"

She sucked in a deep breath. "Well, okay. If you insist. But are you sure your parents won't mind if we bring Hero?"

"Why should they mind? It's not like he's going to be up running around through the house."

"But you said they never allowed you to have a dog."

He laughed. "We're not moving Hero in with them. He's only going for a visit! Are you looking for excuses so you won't have to go with me?"

"No! I'm flattered that you've invited me. I just don't want to be the cause of any trouble."

"Take it from me. There won't be any trouble." He took the carton of slaw from her hand and placed a big spoonful of it on his plate. "We'll plan to leave early Saturday morning. Okay?"

"O—okay, I guess." *What am I doing?*

❧

The week went even better than either of them had hoped. Diane got along fine with Hero during the day, and during evenings, both Valene and Jordan cared for him. Nights, Jordan took over while Valene slept in his condo. Each day the dog showed improvement, and by Friday evening, he was beginning to stand, bearing his own weight with the help of the towel.

"I'm not so sure we should be taking Hero to your parents' house tomorrow," Valene said as she spread out a fresh layer of paper in the dog's bed. "They may not appreciate his messes."

"Don't be silly. We'll both be there to take care of him. I'll toss a couple big bags of paper and a spray can of air freshener in the Avalanche. He'll be fine."

She stood, then fastened the twist tie around the top of the big bag. "You look cute sitting there on the sofa with Hero on your lap."

He gave her a silly grin. "I know this sounds stupid, but I enjoy holding him like this. I can feel his heart beating against my arm. Remember how he struggled those first few times when I tried to lift him? He doesn't do that anymore. I get the feeling he trusts me, and I like that feeling."

She placed the bag in the closet and sat down beside him. "Of course, he trusts you. You've been there for him ever since the accident." She gave his side a jab with her elbow. "He knows you like him. He's watched you clean up his messes!"

He gave her a melancholy look. "Being with Hero these past couple of weeks has made me realize how much I missed by not having a dog when I was a kid. Believe me, when I have kids, they're gonna have a dog. A big one. Like Hero."

She felt herself on the verge of tears. "Oh, Jordan, you've never had the opportunity to be around the real Hero. You've only seen him like this. Totally helpless. I wish you could've seen him when he. . ." Her voice cracked with emotion. "When he. . ." She couldn't say the words.

Jordan freed one hand and pulled her head onto his shoulder. "I know. You don't have to say it. We both know he'll never be able to run and jump like he did before, but the doc said he'd be able to get around fine. We should be thankful for that much. It—it could have been worse. We could've lost him."

She relaxed against his shoulder. It felt good to be able to share her feelings with someone and have them understand. "Thanks, Jordan, for being here."

"I'm right where I want to be, and I promise you, I'll be here until Hero is as well as he's going to get."

Valene's heart clenched. *As well as he's going to get? What about after that? Does that mean you're going to leave us then? Go back to your life and forget about us?*

Jordan gathered Hero up in his arms and stood, leaving Valene on the sofa alone, plagued by unanswered questions.

"Well, I think it's about time this old boy takes his pill and goes to bed. I'd like to head for La Jolla by nine."

"It's not too late, Jordan. You can still change your mind and go by yourself. I won't mind. Really."

"And not take you with me? Forget it. If you don't go, I don't go. Your call."

"But they're expecting you."

"They sure are! So what is it? Go, or stay?"

"You're putting me on the spot, you know."

"I know. But I want you with me. You and Hero."

"Alright, but remember, I'm not a sparkling conversational-ist like my sister."

"All I ask is that you be yourself, and everyone will love you."

❧

Valene nearly choked as they turned onto a magnificent, flower-lined, circular drive in front of a lovely, Spanish-style mansion. "Te—tell me this isn't your parents' home!"

"You don't like it?"

"Of course, I like it. I've never been to such a grand place. Oh, Jordan, why didn't you tell me?"

He stopped the pickup in front of the ornate, iron-railed porch and gave her a blank stare. "Tell you what?"

"That you were raised in such elegant surroundings! You should never have brought me here."

"Why?"

Before she could answer, the door opened and a uniformed butler stepped out.

"Hi, Henry," Jordan sang out as he shook hands with the man. "Good to see you." He turned to Valene. "This is my friend, Valene Zobel."

Henry bowed low as Valene scooted out of the Avalanche. "It's very nice to meet you, Ms. Zobel." Then turning to Jordan, he asked, "May I get your bags, Sir?"

Jordan shook his head. "Later. Where are my parents?"

"In the solarium, Sir, reading the morning paper."

Jordan opened the truck's back door and carefully lifted Hero out.

Henry's eyes widened. "Oh, Sir. I don't think your parents knew you were bringing a dog."

"They'll find out soon enough!" He motioned for Valene to follow and headed toward the door.

She went along, but her heart wasn't in it. *Why didn't he tell me?*

The foyer took her breath away as they entered. Everything was black marble except for one wall completely covered by mirror. She wanted to turn around and run away as fast as she could. She would have, except that she couldn't leave Hero behind and she couldn't break her promise to Jordan.

They crossed through a large room, what she assumed to be the living room. Unlike the foyer, everything in it was white. White damask sofas, white pillows, white ceiling-to-floor drapery, white carpets. The only color in the room came from a lighted painting of a conquistador and several potted palms.

"Coming?" Jordan called over his shoulder.

"Yes, right behind you." She followed him down a long hall swathed in a deep scarlet flocked wallpaper, then entered a wonderful, sunlit room filled with plants of every sort. In the center of the room on heavily-upholstered, high-backed, white wicker chairs sat two glamorous-looking people who had to be Jordan's parents: a man, who looked much like Jordan despite his well-trimmed gray hair, and a woman dressed in a multicolored, floral caftan, who looked as if she'd just stepped out of the city's most elegant salon.

"Jordan, good. You made it. We've been waiting for you," his father said, leaping to his feet.

His mother moved a bit more slowly, seeming to size up the situation before rising. She looked from Hero to Valene, and back to Hero. "What is that?" she asked, pointing to the dog, without so much as a "hello" to her son.

"This is Hero," Jordan said, smiling as proudly as if he owned the dog.

The woman made a face and turned her head away, as if just the sight of the injured dog was repulsive.

"And you are?" she asked, turning to Valene with an expression not much different than she'd given Hero.

"Valene," Valene said timidly, feeling very awkward.

Jordan moved quickly to her side. "Mom, Dad. This is my new friend, Valene Zobel. Valene, these are my parents, Margaret and Colin Young."

"What are you doing with that mongrel?" Mrs. Young asked, turning her attention back to Hero, barely acknowledging Valene's existence.

"Long story. I'll tell you all about it later." Jordan moved to a brightly colored chintz sofa and carefully laid Hero on its cushions. "Right now, I want to fix up a place for Hero."

His mother flew to his side. "Don't put him on the furniture!"

"I'm only going to lay him here until I can fix up a bed for him," Jordan said, smiling at his mother as innocently as a child. "Valene can sit with him. He won't fall off."

"I'm not worried about him falling off! I don't want him there! He'll get it dirty!"

Jordan frowned, as if he couldn't fathom what she was saying. "He's not dirty. The poor dog's been having water therapy everyday. I doubt if there's a speck of dirt on him."

"I can't believe you'd bring a dog into our home, Jordan," his mother said haughtily, pointing her finger in his face. "You know how your father and I—"

"Don't bring me in on this," Colin Young interjected quickly. "You're the one who would never allow pets."

"Get him out of here immediately, Jordan. I do not want him in this house." Margaret Young's face was red with anger.

Jordan scooped Hero up in his arms. "Either Hero stays or we leave. Which is it, Mother?"

"Come on, Margaret. It's only for the weekend," Colin said, slipping an arm about his wife. "Surely it won't hurt to have that dog around for two days. You don't want Jordan to leave, do you?"

All eyes turned to Margaret.

"Well, if he must stay, I guess it will be alright, but I do not want that dog on my furniture!"

Jordan's scowl relaxed a bit. "Fine. I'll keep him off your precious furniture, if that'll make you happy."

"I take it you plan for your little friend to stay for the weekend?" Margaret asked, turning to glare at Valene.

"I thought you told her I was coming with you," Valene whispered, feeling very unwelcome.

"I did," he whispered back.

"When you said you were bringing a friend, Jordan, I assumed it was a male friend," his mother said coolly.

"Male. Female. What difference does it make? You have plenty of guest rooms," he replied indifferently.

"The problem is, Jordan, since I thought you were bringing one of your single, male friends, I've invited Melany Carlson to join us. You and Melany made such a cute couple. I think she thought the two of you would get married someday. She's bringing a friend along for your guest, or at least the guest I'd thought you were bringing. I certainly don't want to have to call and tell them not to come at this late hour."

Jordan shook his head and frowned. "Mother, why'd you invite Melany? You know we were never that serious. You should have asked me first."

"And you should've told me your weekend guest was that woman!" his mother shot back, her hands on her hips.

"Valene is more than 'that woman.' I'd appreciate it if you'd call her by her name!"

"Maybe I'd better leave." Valene's insides were shaking, and she was suddenly sick to her stomach. She'd never been in a situation like this before, and she felt sorry for Jordan.

"No, Valene. If you go, I go!"

His mother's expression softened a bit. "No, Valerie, stay.

You're Jordan's guest. It's too late to do anything about it now."

Jordan bristled visibly. "Her name is Valene, not Valerie, Mother."

"Look," Colin said in a calming voice, raising his palms toward all of them. "Let's not make a big deal out of this. We have a nice dinner party planned for tonight." He turned to Valene. "We're glad to have you here, Valene, despite the way it looks. I think my wife was just unnerved by having Jordan bring your dog in here. She's never liked animals of any kind. I do hope you'll forgive her."

Valene nodded, not sure what to say.

His father gave both her and his son a warm smile. "Jordan, why don't you and Valene go fix up a place for the dog, either in your room or Valene's. She can use the guest room next to yours. I'll have Henry get your bags."

Jordan shot an icy glance toward his mother. "You okay with this?"

She tilted her chin haughtily. "Yes, I suppose so. It seems you give me no choice."

"No 'suppose so,' Mother. I'd appreciate either a direct yes or no."

"Yes, it's fine with me. Both of you may stay."

Jordan gave his father a wink, then turned to Valene with a smile that told her everything was going to be okay. "Come on, Valene. Let's get Hero settled."

Jordan asked Henry to serve a light lunch on the patio, next to the pool, after learning his mother was playing bridge that afternoon and his father was scheduled for a business meeting with one of his cronies.

After Jordan placed Hero on the ground beside them, the two watched as the big dog stretched his body out full-length, obviously enjoying the sun's warmth on his stiffened hips.

"This is so beautiful," Valene said dreamily as she looked

around the spacious grounds. "What fun you must've had growing up here, climbing these magnificent old trees. I'll bet you had a tire swing in that one over there."

"Are you kidding? My mother let me have a tire swing? It would've cluttered up her yard. She'd never allow it. As far as climbing the trees, ha! Not a chance! I might've damaged one of the limbs, and it would have thrown off the symmetry of the garden. You wouldn't believe what my parents pay their Japanese gardener to keep it looking like this."

After praying silently, Valene nibbled on her crab salad, thinking how much fun she and Vanessa had during their growing-up years. They'd spent much of their childhood climbing trees, building crude tree houses, and digging in the backyard. Apparently Jordan hadn't been allowed to enjoy those same delightful pleasures.

"I'm sorry bringing me here has caused so much trouble," Valene said, remembering the look of displeasure on his mother's face when she'd seen her standing at Jordan's side.

"Don't worry about it. My mother thrives on trouble. She's never been a very happy woman."

"Why? She seems to have everything she could ever want."

"Got me! No matter how much they have, it's never enough. She always wants more, and fortunately with my father's income, she can have it. Maybe if he didn't pamper her like he does, she'd appreciate things more." He shrugged. "Don't get me wrong. I love my mother. But to be honest, sometimes I don't like her. She can be very rude and demanding, but you've learned that by experience, haven't you?"

She nodded as she let out a big sigh. "Yes, I have."

"Well, you'll only have to put up with her until tomorrow. Actually, I think she's a little frightened of you."

Her palm went to her chest. "Me? Why would she be frightened of me?"

"Because I've never brought a woman home before. I'm sure we have her wondering about our relationship. Remember? I told you my life has been planned out since I was a child. Getting serious with a woman before I leave the navy has never been a part of that plan."

"But we don't have a relationship."

He grinned as he forked up a bite of salad. "Sure we do. Haven't we been great friends since the day we took Hero to the vet's?"

"Yes, we have," she said, knowing that on her part at least, they were more than just friends.

"But she doesn't know that. I'm sure she thinks there's something serious going on between us. I kinda like the idea of keeping her guessing."

"Oh, I see." Disappointment rippled through her body.

They finished their lunch, then strolled through the majestic gardens, with Jordan carrying Hero in his arms. They sat in the frilly wrought-iron gazebo for more than an hour, each reminiscing about their childhood to the other.

Finally, Valene glanced at her watch. "It's nearly five. Didn't you say dinner was at six?"

"Actually, cocktails are at six. Dinner is at seven."

Valene winced at his words. "Cocktails? I don't drink!"

"Don't worry about it. I'm sure they'll have some soft drinks too. I guess we'd better get back to the house. You'll want some time to get ready," Jordan said, carefully scooping Hero up in his arms.

"I hope the dress I brought will be appropriate."

He grinned. "I'm sure whatever you brought will be just fine. It's only dinner."

"I wouldn't want to embarrass you."

"You could never embarrass me." Jordan turned to her with a giggle. "Did you see that?"

She looked around but didn't see anything unusual.

"Don't look up, but my mother is standing on the balcony off their bedroom, watching us."

"She is?" Valene did her best to keep her eyes from wandering upward, but it was hard.

"Let's give her something to think about. Try not to look surprised. I'm going to kiss you. You ready?"

Valene thought her heart would stop beating. "I–I guess."

Jordan carefully placed Hero on the stone walkway, then pulled Valene into his arms and kissed her with a long, lingering kiss, the kind you see in the movies, then looked into her eyes and kissed her again. "Wow," he said, finally pulling away from her, "that was great! Wanna do it again?"

She couldn't think of a witty thing to say. Her heart was fluttering so rapidly she could barely catch her breath.

"Now," he said, taking her hand in his, "look into my eyes and smile. Pretend like we're having an intimate conversation."

"Oh, Jordan, are you sure we should be deceiving her like this?"

He kissed her cheek, then let go of her hand. "Why not? It'll give her something new to brood over." He carefully picked Hero up, and they continued on into the house.

❧

Valene showered in the amazing glassed-in shower. She'd never seen such a big shower, and she was intrigued by the brass serpent-head faucets. She dried her hair with the room's dryer instead of the one she'd brought, trying to fashion it into a style she thought might be more appropriate for the dreaded evening with the Youngs.

Somehow, the dress she'd liked so well in the store looked frumpy to her now, and she wished she'd had Vanessa there to pick one out for her. Unlike her, her sister always seemed to know the right thing to wear.

She applied her makeup meticulously, tugged on her pantyhose, and slipped into her dress before standing in front of the mirrored closet doors for one final check. *I should've gone for that sleeveless, plain black dress and borrowed Mom's pearls. I hate this ridiculous thing! I look like I'm going to a 4-H banquet! Whatever was I thinking of when I bought this childish-looking get-up? Well, it's too late now. Other than the clean pair of jeans and the T-shirt I brought to wear tomorrow, there's no other choice.*

She slipped into her shoes and sat down on the rose satin love seat, nervously wringing her hands until a knock sounded on her door right at six.

"Hey, you look fantastic!" Jordan stepped back, giving her a full appraisal. "Ready?"

She nodded. "As ready as I'll ever be. It's not too late, Jordan. I don't mind staying in my room. You can go on down there by yourself and have dinner with your friends. I won't be the least bit offended, and I know it'd make your mother happy." She gestured toward the sleeping dog. "Besides, I really don't think we should leave him up here alone."

He held out his hand. "Don't worry about Hero. Remember that Japanese gardener I told you about? He's agreed to stay up here with Hero until we get back. He should be here any minute." He let out a chuckle. "Maybe he'll even teach Hero to bark in Japanese."

"You're one in a million, Jordan Young." She slipped her hand in his. The guy thought of everything.

Before he had time to come up with another clever remark, the gardener appeared. Jordan gave him a few instructions, then, holding Valene's arm, ushered her down the stairs and into the solarium, where the cocktails were being served. His father lifted his glass and gestured to them when they came into the room. His mother only offered a quick, disgusted glance, without so much as acknowledging she'd seen them. She was too caught up visiting with an attractive couple who looked as though they could have been movie stars attending an award function. Margaret Young almost looked like a movie star herself in her lime green pants suit with a huge red lily emblazoned on one side in bright red and green sequins. A quick glance around the room and Valene knew she was underdressed by far. Every other woman in the room either sparkled, glittered, or glowed.

"Let's go say hello to Mother," Jordan said, gently tugging Valene in her direction.

Do we have to? she mouthed silently so Jordan wouldn't hear her. If she had her way, she'd never have to meet Margaret Young face-to-face again, but that, too, was wishful thinking.

Jordan's mother turned away from her guests when he and Valene approached. Valene felt criticism in the woman's eyes as they scanned her from the top of her head to the soles of her shoes. It was obvious Margaret Young was not pleased by her appearance.

Valene clung tightly to Jordan's arm.

"Whatever did you do with that dreadful dog?" his mother asked, ignoring Valene.

Jordan took in a deep breath. "You needn't worry about him. He's being taken cared for by someone quite competent."

Margaret curled her finger, and instantly, a young woman dressed in a black uniform topped by a white apron appeared with a drink tray. "What would you like, Valerie?"

Jordan gave his mother a frosty look. "Her name is Valene, Mother. Is that so hard to remember?"

"I'll just have ginger ale, thank you."

Mrs. Young stepped back and, with a raised brow of amusement, gave her a ridiculing smile. "If you say so."

Turning to her son she asked, "Wherever did you find this woman, Jordan? In a convent?"

"No, Mother. I didn't." He turned to the server. "Oh, and make that two ginger ales."

"That's an interesting little frock you're wearing." Margaret reached out and touched Valene's sleeve. "Polyester, isn't it?"

Valene's first thought was to respond with, "No, it's burlap," but she'd never want to embarrass Jordan, and the rude woman was his mother. Instead she smiled sweetly and said, "Yes, I like polyester. It takes very little care."

"Well, it's—it's charming," Margaret said, drawling out her words. "Polyester is quite durable, I've heard."

"Did someone get your drink orders?" Colin Young asked as he joined them.

"Oh, yes," Margaret said, her face seeming to be frozen in the familiar smirk. "They've both ordered ginger ale. I think our son has reformed."

Colin smiled as he lifted his glass and gave them all a wink. "Good idea. That's what I'm having."

Margaret latched onto Jordan's arm and pulled him toward a group of four ladies standing by a brilliant display of red geraniums and white chrysanthemums. "Look who's here, Jordan," she said, nearly pushing him into the petite little blond squeezed into a dress at least a size too small for her.

The woman spun around and gave Jordan a coquettish smile. "Jordan, how nice to see you again. You must come over and play tennis with me while you're home. Maybe tomorrow morning?"

Jordan turned and reached a hand toward Valene. "Melany Carlson, meet Valene Zobel. Valene is my guest for the weekend."

The woman's eyes widened. "But, I thought—"

"I'm sorry if there was a misunderstanding, Melany.

Apparently Mother thought the guest I was bringing was another man." He gave her a friendly smile. "Now if you'll excuse us, we have a dog to check on before dinner."

Melany gave him a puzzled look. "A dog?"

Jordan grinned as he pulled Valene toward the door. "A very special dog."

"Nice to have met you, Miss Carlson," Valene said quickly as Jordan led her away.

"You really didn't want that ginger ale, did you?" he asked as he pulled her through the door of the solarium and headed toward the room where the gardener was staying with Hero.

She shook her head with a laugh, glad to be leaving the cocktail party sooner than expected. "No, I'd much rather check on Hero."

A few minutes before seven, the two of them rejoined the others in the massive dining room. The table was splendidly set with sparkling china and crystal. Small vases of fresh flowers marked each place setting.

Still clinging to Valene's hand, Jordan quickly made a circle around the table, checking the name on each place card. When he found his mother had arranged for him to sit across the table from Valene and next to Melany, he quickly switched the cards. "Shh, no one will ever know."

"Your mother will," she whispered back.

Once everyone was seated, Valene discreetly bowed her head to pray.

"Aren't you feeling well, Valerie?" Margaret asked. "Perhaps you'd like to go to your room and lie down."

"Valene is praying, Mother," Jordan explained, sounding almost proud. "It's what some of us do before we eat."

Valene quickly finished her prayer and smiled up at him.

"Oh," his mother said with a tilt of her head. "I didn't realize Valerie—"

"Valene!" Jordan said in an exaggerated tone. "How many times do I have to tell you? Her name is Valene!"

"What I was saying was. . ." Margaret glared at her son. "I didn't realize Valene was one of those."

"And just what do you mean by 'one of those'?"

"You know perfectly well what I mean."

"I'm a Christian too, Mother. You know that, although you choose to ignore it."

The room was suddenly filled with silence as every guest looked toward Margaret and Jordan.

"I propose a toast!" Colin rose quickly and loudly rattled his spoon against his glass. "To family, good friends, business associates, and neighbors. May each of us prosper!"

Everyone lifted their glasses and added a "Hear, hear!" Even Jordan and Valene lifted their glasses—their water glasses.

"Enjoy your dinner!" Colin said with a bow toward his guests.

Valene paused before eating her salad, waiting to see which fork everyone else used before picking up her own. The vegetables were nice and crisp, just the way she liked them, although some of them she didn't recognize.

When the butler came around with the basket of rolls, she reached in and took one.

"We have servants to do that for you, Valerie," Margaret said, chastising her and pointing to the ornate silver tongs in the man's hand.

Jordan reached past her and took a roll from the basket with a grin as his mother grimaced.

Valene had never been so uncomfortable. Every bite she took was sheer agony. What if she dropped something on the pristine tablecloth?

"Relax," Jordan whispered, as he leaned toward her. "Don't let her get to you."

She smiled back and reached for her water glass, hoping the cool liquid would dissolve the lump in her throat. But her nervousness caused her aim to miss, and instead of picking up the water glass, she knocked it over. A river of water and ice flowed across the table, a portion of it dropping onto Melany's short dress. Others seated in its path jumped quickly to their feet, throwing their napkins onto the table to stop the flow.

"I'm—I'm so sorry. I never meant to—"

Jordan tossed his own napkin onto the puddle and wrapped a consoling arm about her. "It's okay. Don't feel bad. The servants will have it cleaned up in a second. Accidents happen."

"I think I'd better go to my room." Valene tried to stand but Jordan's hold on her tightened.

"No, you're staying right here with me," he whispered as he held her tight.

She sat rigid, feeling more foolish than ever before in her life. *Why, oh why, did I let Jordan talk me into coming? Or is it God's will that I be here? Maybe He's trying to make me see I'd never fit into Jordan's world!*

The rest of the dinner went without mishap. Afraid of making another mistake, Valene merely toyed with her food.

By the time dessert came, she had calmed down and was able to almost enjoy the rich chocolate cheesecake garnished with whipped cream and fresh strawberries.

"You have a bit of whipped cream on your chin, Valerie," Mrs. Young said, pointing her long finger.

Valene grabbed at her napkin. "Ah, thank you."

Jordan squinted as he bent close to her. "I didn't see any whipped cream."

There probably wasn't any, Valene thought, giving the woman a quick glance. *Just another one of her ploys to embarrass me.*

Jordan stood and pulled Valene up with him. "It was nice to see all of you again, but I'm afraid Valene and I are going to have to excuse ourselves. We have an ailing dog upstairs, and we want to go check on him. Enjoy your evening."

Mrs. Young grabbed his arm as he passed. "But Jordan. Vladimir is going to entertain us in the parlor. I know how you love hearing him play the piano. Perhaps Valerie could stay with that dog."

"Val-lene," Jordan said, emphasizing her name. "We both need to check on Hero. He's much too heavy for her to lift. We'll see you in the morning."

With one final wave to his parents and their guests, he led Valene out of the dining room. "Sorry, I put you through that."

"She hates me, Jordan. I know she does. I don't belong here. This world is completely foreign to me. But I do appreciate your father. He's been very kind."

"Nights like this, I don't know how he can live with her. I suppose they do have their good moments. Sometimes I think Mother is Father's trophy. She's normally a wonderful hostess to his business associates, and she gives great parties which can be a real asset to his business."

"She's quite a bit younger than he is, isn't she?"

"Oh, yes, about fifteen years younger. I imagine her age and her good looks are what attracted him."

When they reached Valene's room, the gardener reported on how the evening had gone. "Hero did fine," he said. "He's a nice dog."

Jordan pulled out his wallet and gave the man a few bills, thanked him, and shut the door behind him. "Looks like he got along okay without us."

Valene stooped down beside Hero and patted his head. "Oh, oh."

Jordan shoved his wallet into his pocket and bent down beside her. "Oh, Hero, why didn't you do that when that guy was here to clean you up?"

"I'll do it," Valene said, slipping out of her shoes.

"No, it's my turn. You did it last time."

He pulled off his jacket and began rolling up his sleeves. "We'll both do it."

They'd no more than started the clean-up job when someone rapped on the door.

eight

"Door's open," Jordan called out as he lifted Hero from his bed of paper.

"I've come to apologize—" Colin's eyes flitted from Jordan cradling the dog, to Valene holding a huge bag filled with shredded paper. He reared back with a laugh. "Now, that is a sight!"

"You needn't apologize for Mother," Jordan said with a half-smile, awkwardly holding the offensive dog away from his shirt. "She needs to apologize for herself."

"You know your mother well enough, Son, to know that will never happen." He stared at Hero. "What happened to him anyway?"

"He's this way because of me, Dad. I was driving across the parking lot at my condo and accidentally hit him with my truck. He has a fractured pelvis. As you can see, he's pretty helpless. Right now, he requires care around the clock."

The man patted Hero on the head. "Oh, Jordan, how awful! I can see why you're so concerned about him. Will he ever be able to walk again?"

Jordan nodded. "Yes, he's getting better every day, but his hips will always be stiff. We've been giving him water baths as therapy. The doc said he should be able to stand by himself before long. Meantime, he'll have to drag his hind end around. We try to help him by putting him on a towel and assisting him. He's a good dog."

"I had no idea. No wonder you wanted to bring him along."

"That's not the half of it. I nearly hit the six-year-old boy

Hero was chasing. If I hadn't hit the brakes in time, I might have injured or killed a child. Instead I hit Hero."

"I'm proud of you, Son, for facing up to your responsibilities. And I'm glad you brought Valene along."

"She's become a good friend through all of this. We enjoy each other's company."

Valene, still holding the bag of paper, stepped forward with a smile. "Thank you, Mr. Young. Your words mean a lot to me. You've raised a fine son."

Mr. Young's smile left. "I'm afraid I can't take much credit for Jordan's upbringing, and neither can my wife. We left much of his care to our housekeeper. We were both too busy with things that really didn't matter. But I'm quite proud of Jordan and the man he has become."

"You should be proud. He's one of the nicest and finest men I've ever met."

"Hey, you two. Don't talk about me like I'm not here!"

Colin's smile returned. "I'll let you get back to that dog. Hero? Is that what you said his name was?"

Valene nodded. "Yes, I know it's a silly name for a dog, but it seems to suit him."

"I like the name. This world would be a better place if we had more heroes. See you both at breakfast?"

"Yes, Sir. We'll be there," Jordan told him. "I'd shake hands with you, but—"

The two men laughed.

"Carry on with your cleaning project. I'd better get back to your mother before she comes looking for me."

"I like him," Valene said as the door closed behind Jordan's father.

"Good. I can tell he likes you too."

☙

Colin and Margaret were already seated at the table in the

breakfast room when Jordan and Valene came down the next morning.

"Well, how did Hero sleep?" Mr. Young asked as Jordan and Valene took their chairs at the table.

"He went to sleep right after Jordan gave him his Rimadyl and slept the rest of the night without making a sound.

"Good! You must keep me posted on his recovery."

"I do hope you're keeping that dog off the furniture, Jordan. I've heard an animal's smell is almost impossible to get out of upholstery." His mother raised a well-arched brow. "Carpeting too."

"I brought a large piece of plastic sheeting to place on the floor under a double layer of cardboard. I doubt your carpet will smell," Jordan said, seeming almost amused. "I even brought a can of room freshener. I'll be sure to give the guest room a good spritzing before we leave. And for your information, Hero has not been on your precious furniture."

The maid brought in their breakfast. Valene opted for juice, coffee, and a bagel with cream cheese, while Jordan went for the whole works—eggs, bacon, biscuits, and gravy.

"Too bad you had to leave to take care of that dreadful dog last night, Jordan. We had a wonderful time visiting with our guests," his mother said, "and Vladimir's playing was astounding, as usual. Did you know Melany is going to Paris next month?"

Jordan dabbed at his mouth with his napkin. "No, I didn't know that."

"I think this will be her third trip abroad this year." Margaret took a sip of juice, then turned her attention toward Valene. "Have you been to Paris lately?"

"No. I've never been to Paris."

"Oh, what a pity. There are so many amazing things to do in Paris. Have you been to Rome? I love Rome. The Italian fashions are to die for."

"No, I've never been to Rome. In fact, I've barely been out of California," Valene confessed reluctantly.

"That's too bad. Traveling is such a stimulating way to broaden one's horizons."

"I'm sure it is."

Margaret reached over, her fingers cupping Valene's wrist. "I don't recall you mentioning your parents' business."

"They don't have a business. My dad will retire from the phone company in a few years. My mother has never worked outside our home, except for an occasional baby-sitting job."

Mrs. Young's eyes widened. "Really? The phone company? Well, I suppose someone has to do those things, or we wouldn't be able to have phones."

"Her parents are great people. I've met them. Valene has a twin sister, but she's been on her honeymoon, so I haven't met her yet."

"A twin? That must be interesting," his father said.

Valene smiled with pride. "It is! She and I have always been close. I'm afraid I'm going to have trouble adjusting to the fact that she's married now."

"Jordan, do you remember the Gallagers?" his mother asked, interrupting. "Mr. Gallager sold his investment company recently, and they've bought the old Kilmer place. They have a lovely daughter about your age. She's anxious to meet you. I think the two of you will have a lot in common."

Jordan speared a hunk of biscuit and gravy with his fork and twirled it in the air. "Sorry, Mother. Not interested."

"Jordan, mind your manners," his mother said sharply.

"Hey, Dad, how's the golf game going? Won any tournaments lately?"

Colin took his last sip of coffee and placed his cup in the

saucer. "I'm not any better at golf now than I was ten years ago, but I have to say, I've made some pretty good deals on the course. Seems men are more relaxed when they're playing golf. Just last week, one of my golf partners signed a good contract with our firm, right there on the ninth hole. The caddy had to loan him a pen."

"Sounds to me like you'd better keep on playing golf!" Jordan said with a wink as he spread jam on a fresh biscuit.

"You need to spend more time at the office with me, Jordan," his father said, his expression turning serious. "It won't be too many more years before you'll be taking over the business. You need to keep abreast of what's going on."

"I've got a few years yet, Dad. Don't rush me."

"Jordan tells me you were a navy man too," Valene said, feeling the need to participate in the conversation.

"I was. Graduated from Annapolis like Jordan did, but he graduated with honors. I didn't."

"He's being modest," Jordan said, beaming at his father. "I barely beat him out. You ought to see his awards."

"You're being quiet, my dear," Colin commented to Margaret.

"I'm a bit weary. I didn't sleep well last night. I may take an aspirin and go back to bed."

Jordan placed his napkin on the table. "Well, you needn't worry about entertaining us. Valene and I are heading home as soon as we get things loaded into the Avalanche."

"Why do you drive that hideous vehicle?" his mother asked, pushing away her dishes. "It's ghastly."

"Hey, don't talk about my truck that way. That's what all us jocks drive these days."

"I wish you wouldn't call yourself a jock. The word has such a vulgar connotation to it."

"I like that truck. It serves my purpose well, and if I ever get stuck in a snowstorm—"

"In California? You rarely go up in the mountains, and that's the only place you might need it around here."

"Ah, but having it gives me the option in case I ever decide I want to."

Valene had to smile to herself as she listened to them bantering back and forth. How much his mother and father had missed by not spending time with him when he was a boy.

"Well, good-bye, you two. Been good to see you both. We'd better be hitting the road," Jordan said finally.

Colin held out his hand. "Good-bye, Son. Drive carefully."

Margaret lifted a cheek toward Jordan and held it there until he finally kissed it. "Good-bye, Jordan."

❧

Although Jordan apologized profusely for his mother's insolent behavior, Valene found it hard to forgive her. She'd never been around someone like Margaret Young, and she wasn't sure she ever wanted to see the woman again. Yet Valene knew that if she ever wanted to be near Jordan, she must recognize that Margaret came with the package. The woman would always be his mother.

"How come you're so quiet?" Jordan asked, reaching over to take her hand.

"Been thinking."

"About what? Your wonderful, entertaining weekend at the Young house?"

"Something like that."

They rode along quietly the rest of the way with Jordan occasionally trying to get a conversation started, but to no avail. Valene didn't feel like talking.

When they reached her condo, he gathered Hero up in his arms and carried him inside before going back for Valene's suitcase and the dog's bed.

Once Hero was settled, Jordan bent and kissed Valene on the cheek. "Thanks for going with me. I had no idea things would be that bad. I know my mother embarrassed you, and I'm sorry. You were a good sport, but I should never have put you in that position. I guess by being away from her as much as I have since I went off to Annapolis, I'd forgotten how vindictive she can be."

Valene dropped down on the sofa with a deep sigh. "This has got to end, Jordan."

He sat down beside her and slipped an arm about her shoulders. "What has to end?"

"Us. Our relationship."

"Why? I thought we were getting along so well."

"I know we're only friends, but can't you see? Other than Hero, we have nothing in common. Your world is wealth, prestige, and excitement. I'm a commoner. A nobody."

"I don't see what any of that has to do with us being friends, and besides, you're wrong. You're selling yourself short, as usual."

She motioned toward the door. "I think you'd better go. Hero's getting along fine now. You've done more than your part in helping him get well. Between Diane and me, we should be able to take care of him until he's able to stand on his own. Go back to your world. Forget about us."

"What if I don't want to forget about you?"

"It's for your own good, Jordan. You've put off way too many things these past couple of weeks to spend time with us. I don't want you to sacrifice any longer."

"Who said I was sacrificing? Have you heard me complain?"

She pulled away and crossed her arms defiantly. "I really don't want to see you anymore. I have my life to live too."

"You really want me to leave? You're sure?"

"Quite sure."

"You realize if I walk out that door, I may never come back?"

She wanted to throw herself into his arms and beg him to stay with her forever, but she couldn't. "Yes, I know."

"Have I done something to offend you? Are you mad at me?"

"No, of course not."

"Can't you see I care for you? You're much more to me than a friend."

How much more, Jordan? Am I just another one of your groupies? Like Melany? Will you cast me aside someday like you probably did to her?

"Valene? Did you hear me?"

"I heard you, Jordan. Please go."

"Okay! If that's the way you want it. We'll do it your way. If you need any help with Hero, give me a call. Otherwise you won't be hearing from me. But remember, Valene, this was your idea. Not mine."

Jordan grabbed his jacket from the chair, bent and patted Hero one last time, and stormed out, slamming the door behind him.

Valene rose and walked slowly to the door, pressing her cheek against it as her tears flowed. "I love you, Jordan, but you've never said you love me. You're out of my league. I've known that from the start. I can't set myself up for a broken heart."

Lord, I need Your help. Fill my heart with the peace that only You can give.

Just then the phone rang, and Valene rushed to answer it, hoping it was Jordan.

"Hi, Sis," a cheery voice said on the other end of the line. "Nathan and I are back from our honeymoon. I'm coming over. I want to meet that hunk Mom said is helping you take care of Hero. You've got to tell me all about him."

"No, don't—"

"Hey, I know you're busy, but I'm coming. Nathan is going

to stay here with Mom and Dad. I'll be there in half an hour."

Before Valene could explain why she couldn't introduce her sister to Jordan, Vanessa hung up.

❧

"You what?" Vanessa screamed at Valene. They'd been sitting on the sofa for a full hour. The first half hour, Vanessa spent telling Valene all about the honeymoon. The second half hour, Valene told Vanessa about the accident and everything leading up to the minute she'd told Jordan to get out of her life.

"I told him to leave. Don't you see, Van, even if he felt the same way about me as I feel about him, there are too many obstacles in the way. Right now, the navy is his life, and he has no intention of leaving it for probably another four years. There's no place for a wife in his plans. I'd never fit into his world. His mother hates me."

Vanessa leaned back into the sofa and clasped her hands behind her head. "You, dear sister, have a problem."

"But Vanessa, I never knew losing Jordan was going to hurt this much. He's only been gone a few hours, and I'm miserable."

"I know, Kiddo. I know, and I'll be praying for the two of you. I hate to leave you, but I promised Nathan I'd be back in two hours. You gonna be alright here by yourself?"

Valene gestured toward Hero, who was trying to pull himself off the bed Jordan had made for him. "I've got Hero. He'll keep me company."

"Call if you need me, and I'll be here in a flash."

"I know that. You've always been there for me. Thanks for coming over. Tell Nathan 'hi' for me, and give Jeff a kiss. I love that boy. Oh, by the way, Jeff left one of his books in my car. It's unlocked. You'd better take it to him."

She watched as the door closed behind her sister before

breaking down and crying until she could cry not more. Jordan was out of her life.

❧

Jordan walked slowly toward his pickup. He wasn't exactly hungry; he just couldn't stand the idea of sitting in that condo one more minute, knowing Valene was just a few doors away. He'd nearly reached it when he noticed her leaning into her car as if trying to retrieve something.

He rushed over, grabbed her by the wrist, and pulled her into his arms. "Are you sure you won't change your mind?"

"You must be Jordan!"

nine

Jordan pushed away from her a bit and stared into her face. "Of course, I'm Jordan. Who else would I be?"

"I'm Vanessa! Valene's twin sister," Vanessa told him with a giggle.

He couldn't believe it. The likeness was uncanny. "Whoops, sorry! I didn't know you were back in town. Have you talked to Valene yet?"

"Yes, I just spent the last hour with her. She told me all about you."

"Did she tell you she told me to get lost?"

Vanessa's smile disappeared. "Yes, she did, but she had her reasons. I'm sure she explained them to you."

"She did, but I just don't get it. I thought we were getting along fine. Then pow! I take her to visit my parents for the weekend, and she turns on me."

Vanessa pulled Jeff's book from the car and closed the door. "I know what she's going through, Jordan. She felt like a misfit at your parents' house. We didn't have all the advantages you had growing up, but we had parents who loved us and did all they could for us. Val felt like the proverbial fish out of water in La Jolla."

He had to make her understand. "But I'm not like my parents. At least, not like my mother. I know she gave Valene a hard time, and I'm sorry. If I'd had any idea Mother would treat her the way she did, I would never have taken her there."

"There were other reasons too. Valene's always wanted to meet Mr. Right, get married, and have children, but she—"

"I want that too, just not now."

"Not for a number of years, from what Valene tells me."

Jordan clasped his hands together and stood staring at her. "Look, I'm a navy pilot. Right now, I couldn't offer anything permanent to any woman. Not even a woman as wonderful as Valene. When I'm out of the country on a mission, I may be gone for months at a time. What kind of a life would that be for her? I'd never want to be married and have a wife and kids to leave behind. No, Sir. As long as I'm in the navy, it's better for everyone if I remain unattached. But I do want to keep up a relationship with Valene." He grinned. "You could put in a good word for me!"

Vanessa gave him a slap on the back. "Sorry, Pal. You're on your own on this one. A woman can't wait forever. Especially a woman like my sister."

"I don't want our relationship to end this way. She's been too good a friend for that."

Vanessa tilted her head as she gazed at him. "I have one question I want to leave with you, and I suggest you give it some serious thought."

"Oh, what?"

"Do you love her?"

With that, she turned and walked to her car, and he was left standing alone in the parking lot.

❧

Although Hero slept fairly well, Valene had a miserable night. She couldn't get her mind off Jordan. Even praying didn't seem to help. Where was that peace God promised to those who love Him?

She routinely took care of Hero's needs, then dressed quickly for work. By the time Diane arrived, Val was ready to head out the door.

At five, when she walked back into her condo, Diane handed her a vase containing a dozen red roses. Their sweet fragrance filled the room. Valene held them close, their velvety pedals caressing her cheek. The attached card bore only a few words: I'm waiting for your call.

Each of the next five days, flowers arrived with the same words on the card. Valene would hold them close and cry. She wanted to call Jordan and thank him and tell him Hero had stood completely on his own for the first time, but she didn't. The ache in her heart hadn't lessened one bit.

By Saturday, she was exhausted and nearly to the point of calling Jordan. Living without him in her life had become unbearable.

Late Sunday afternoon, after she'd given Hero his water therapy and his Rimadyl, she decided enough was enough. She had to see Jordan. She dabbed on a bit of lipstick, ran a comb through her hair, and hurried across the sidewalk to his condo, but no one was home. Disappointed, she started back to her place, when Diane's door opened.

"I heard you knocking. Jordan isn't home. He hasn't been for several days now. I don't know where he is. He asked me to take in his newspaper and his mail until he gets back."

Valene's heart plummeted. Where could he be? Maybe he was staying at the base to avoid seeing her. She thanked Diane and rushed back to Hero.

The next two days dragged by. By the time Valene had given Hero his water therapy, cleaned up the kitchen, and folded two loads of laundry, she was dead tired. She fell down onto her sofa and turned on the eleven o'clock news to check the weather report. But when the lead story came on, she sat up straight and quickly turned up the volume. "A Navy F/A-18 from the San Diego Naval Base has gone down in the Philippines, killing the pilot," the newscaster was saying. "At this time details are limited. The name of the deceased pilot is being withheld until the next of kin can be notified."

Valene went ballistic. That pilot could be Jordan! Why else would he be gone from his condo for five days straight, unless he was on a mission?

Frantically, she dialed Jordan's base apartment. His answering machine picked up, and she listened to the recording of his voice explain he was unable to take calls and to please leave a message.

She hung up quickly and phoned the base switchboard, asking if Jordan Young was on the downed plane.

"Sorry, Ma'am, unless you are a close relative and can verify your identity, we cannot give out that information."

Terrified, Valene began to pace about the room. She had to know if Jordan was dead or alive.

Suddenly, a thought occurred to her. Next of kin! His parents, they'd know! But what if they hadn't been notified yet? She couldn't just call them and ask if the navy had contacted them. They'd be sick with worry. Maybe Jordan was safe somewhere. Maybe sitting in an arena watching a basketball game or playing tennis or. . .

She had to find out. Maybe she could casually ask his parents if they'd talked to him lately. What if his mother answered the phone? Margaret probably wouldn't tell her anything, even if they'd been notified. She had to take a chance and hope his father was the one to answer, or at least the butler.

With fingers almost too nervous to dial, Val called the house in La Jolla.

"Hello."

"Mrs. Young, this is Valene Zobel. I haven't seen Jordan

around his condo for several days, and I've been concerned about him. I thought perhaps maybe he was sick, or—"

"You have no right calling my son. Why don't you leave him alone? I know all about women like you. You find some unsuspecting man you think has money, and you chase after him shamelessly. Stay away from him, do you hear?"

Shocked by the harsh accusations, Valene hung up the phone without responding. Although she was hurt by the woman's words, she was also encouraged. Surely if Mrs. Young had received bad news about Jordan, she wouldn't be answering the phone. She'd be grieving.

In near hysterics, Val stayed up all night, scanning the television channels, hoping for more news about the crash, but most of the comments the newscasters gave were only repeats.

When Diane came over the next morning, Valene told her what she'd heard on the news and that she had decided to take the day off in case the pilot's name was released.

At ten that night when the phone rang, she let the machine pick up, afraid to miss even one second of the local newscast. But when she heard Jordan's voice on the answering machine, she leaped to answer it before he could hang up.

"Oh, Jordan, it's you!" she said, tears blinding her. "I've been so worried. I was afraid that was your plane that crashed." She was sobbing so hard she was afraid he wouldn't be able to make out her words.

"I'm fine. I've been on a short-term training mission all week. I didn't even know about the crash until this evening when we got into port."

"Oh, Jordan, I was so afraid I'd lost you! I love you so much. If anything ever happened to you, I'd—" She stopped midsentence, realizing what she'd said.

"You mean it? You love me?"

"Yes," she said between sobs, "I know you don't love me, but I can't help myself. Outside of God, you're the most important person in my life."

"Oh, but I do love you. That's the main reason I called. The day I talked with Vanessa, she asked me, point-blank, if I loved you. I've never been in love before, Valene. I didn't have a clue as to how it felt or what it was. But when I thought I'd lost you, I realized what I was feeling was indeed love. Nothing means more to me than you. Not flying, not the navy, not my parents, not my future at my family's company. I'd give it all away rather than lose you."

Those were the sweetest words Valene had ever heard, and she was filled with such emotion, all she could do was cry.

"Oh, Valene, you're all I've thought about since we've been apart. I wish I wasn't so far away. I want to hold you in my arms and look into those beautiful blue eyes."

"I–I want that too."

"Look, I won't be home from this mission until Friday. Can we spend the weekend together? Just you and me. . ." He snickered. "And Hero?"

She cupped the phone in her hands, feeling it was her life-line to him. "Oh, yes, I. . .we'd like that."

"How is he, Valene? I've been worried sick about both of you. I should never have let you take care of him by your-self. I'll bet you're exhausted, but I'm going to pamper you when I get home. I promise I'll take care of Hero the whole weekend."

She let out a giggle. "He'll be glad to see you. He's not too crazy about the way I handle him. I've been putting him on the towel and dragging him to the tub."

"I almost didn't call. I was afraid you'd hang up on me. But

I had to hear your voice."

She brushed away a tear and swallowed at a sob. "I'm glad you did. I can't begin to tell you how much I've missed you."

"See you Friday night, Sweetheart."

"I'll be waiting, and Jordan—please be careful flying."

"I love you, Valene. I think I've always loved you."

"I love you too, Jordan. I can't wait to see you."

Valene cradled the phone long after he'd hung up. Jordan was safe, and he loved her! She bowed her head to thank God for answered prayer and for bringing Jordan back to her.

୧ଛ

Jordan smiled as he hung up the phone. He could hardly wait to hold Valene in his arms.

He looked up a number in the directory and dialed the phone. The person he was calling picked up on the second ring.

"Chaplain Abbot."

"This is Jordan Young. I need to talk to you again."

"I'm free now."

"I'll be right there."

୧ଛ

The next few weeks were the happiest ones Valene had ever known, as she and Jordan spent every possible moment together talking on the phone, listening to CDs, holding hands while walking in the park, cuddling in front of the TV, attending the Sunday morning services at her church, and falling deeper in love.

Despite his parents' insistence that he come to La Jolla for Thanksgiving, Jordan opted to spend the holiday with Valene and her family instead, at Nathan and Vanessa's picturesque 1865 saltbox-styled home, the one Nathan had lovingly restored.

After a sumptuous Thanksgiving dinner with all the trimmings, Valene and Jordan broke away from the rest of the family and wandered into the backyard.

"Wow," Jordan said, as they walked through the lush stand of green grass toward a lacy white gazebo surrounded by dozens of colorful chrysanthemum plants. "This is beautiful!"

"Yes, it is beautiful, but nothing like your parents' yard. Umm, don't you love the smell of freshly mown grass?"

They pushed aside one of the vines twining its way around the lovely gazebo and sat down on one of the ornate benches.

"Nathan did all this work himself? My parents have a team of gardeners who take care of their lawn, and it doesn't look much better than this." He leaned back on the bench and crossed his ankles. "It must give him a great deal of satisfaction to know he's restored an 1865 house like he has and to have built this magnificent gazebo. I envy him, being able to work with his hands."

Valene laughed. "He probably envies you being able to fly like you do."

Jordan grinned. "It's a man thing."

He pulled her into his arms and held her close, their foreheads touching as they gazed into each other's eyes.

"I love you, Valene. Will you marry me?"

She pulled back and stared at him. *Marry me? Is that what he said? After all his comments about staying single?*

"I can't promise you an easy life, not yet anyway. Not until I get out of the navy, which might be another four years. But other guys in my squad are married. If they can do it, surely we can if you love me as much as I love you."

She wanted to shout yes! But despite their deep feelings for one another, so many obstacles still stood in their way.

"I don't know, Jordan. You know I love you, and I want so much to say yes." She reached up and gently stroked his cheek. "Marrying you would be a dream come true. But your parents would be furious with you. Especially your mother. She'd never allow you to marry outside of your social circle. You know that. She'd much prefer you marry someone like Melany or Charmaine. Someone with breeding and class. Someone with social graces."

"It's my life, Valene. I can't live it for my parents. I don't want any of those women to be my wife. I want you. I love you. Please say you'll marry me!"

"I want to marry you, Jordan. You know I do! I've told you how much I love you. I nearly went crazy when we broke up. I was miserable without you. But—"

"Look. Let's plan on announcing our engagement at Christmas. That'll give us a month to work out all the kinks. I won't let you go again. We can't let anyone, or anything, stand in our way. We have to be together!"

"You sure about this?" Valene asked. "Marriage is a lifetime commitment. When I marry, it's going to be one of those 'till death do us part' things. No escape! No changing your mind later!"

He kissed the tip of her nose. "That's the way I want it too. I know our love will last a lifetime. Come on, say yes!"

She allowed her slow smile to turn into a broad grin. "Okay. I'll marry you! We'll tell everyone at Christmas. Like you said, that'll give us time to work out all the kinks."

"If I can keep it quiet for that long," he said, his smile radiating his joy. "I'd like to plaster the news on a billboard! Tell everyone I know, you're going to be my wife!"

She threw her arms about his neck, laughing hysterically. "I love you! I love you! I love you!"

When they walked arm-in-arm back into the house from their walk, Vanessa asked, "What's with you two? You look like you've just won the lottery, but I know that can't be so, because neither of you ever buys a ticket."

Jordan grinned. "We've sorta come to an understanding."

❧

The next month passed quickly, as fall turned rapidly to winter, on the calendar, at least. The San Diego area's weather was much the same year round. Bright and sunny.

Valene and Jordan spent a traditional Christmas Eve with her family at her parents' home in Granite Cliff. After the Christmas story had been read from the Bible and all the gifts had been opened, Jordan clapped his hands loudly.

"Since I consider all of you to be my family now, Valene and I would like you to be a part of something special." He dropped to one knee in front of her, taking her hand in his and caressing it as he gazed up at her.

"Valene Zobel, I love you with all my heart, and you've said you love me. I want us to spend the rest of our lives together." He pulled a beautiful diamond solitaire ring from his pocket and placed it on her finger. "Will you marry me?"

Valene's heart leaped with happiness as she circled her arms about Jordan's neck. The day she had hoped for, yes, even prayed for, had come. "Yes, dear Jordan! I'll marry you! I love you with all my heart. My life wouldn't be complete without you."

There wasn't a dry eye in the room, as their loved ones shared in their joy.

Jordan pulled her to her feet and wrapped his arms about her. "I love you, Valene. I'll always love you." Then he kissed her. To Valene, it seemed the world began to swirl around them as her love for him overflowed her heart. Soon she would be his, to have and hold until death.

ॐ

"Remember, Valene," Jordan told her as they stood outside the front door of his parents' home the next morning. "You're marrying me, not my parents. Maybe when they see we're determined, they'll be happy for us."

She leaned her head against his shoulder with a sigh. "I'm so afraid your mother will go through the roof when she finds out we're engaged. I don't want to be the cause of any trouble between you and your parents."

"Hopefully, there won't be any trouble. I made it perfectly clear when I phoned them to say we were going to spend Christmas Day with them that I would not come unless both you and Hero were welcome." His reassuring smile warmed her heart and gave her courage. "Ready?"

She lifted her chin and pasted on a smile. "Ready."

Instead of the butler, Colin himself opened the door. "Merry Christmas, you two!" He threw his arms open wide. "It's so good to have you here."

He shook Jordan's free hand and kissed Valene's cheek. "You too, Hero."

Jordan raised a brow. "Mother wasn't too thrilled when I insisted he come with us."

Colin gave him a wink. "Don't worry about your mother. I'll take care of her."

"Merry Christmas!" Margaret rushed into the foyer, dressed in a flowing red caftan that rustled when she walked, totally ignoring Valene's presence. "I'm so glad you made it, Jordan." She stopped short when she saw Hero.

"Merry Christmas, Mrs. Young" Valene said brightly, trying to ease the tension she'd already begun to feel.

Margaret barely cast a glance over her shoulder before adding a slightly cool, "Merry Christmas."

Colin put an arm about his wife. "I was just telling Jordan and Valene how glad we are to have them here."

Hero let out a slight yelp as Jordan tugged on his leash.

"Surely you don't expect that dog to have free rein of this house!" Margaret's nose wrinkled up as she turned her head away. "Can't you put that dreadful animal outside somewhere, Jordan? Maybe in one of the garages? But don't turn him loose. I don't want him digging in the lawn.

Jordan shook his head and narrowed his eyes. "Look, Mother, I explained all of this to you on the phone. You knew I was bringing Hero. Father has gone out of his way to make us feel welcome. Now either you quit being Miss Hoity-Toity, or we're leaving. Am I making myself clear?"

"You needn't speak to me in that tone of voice," Margaret said, looking hurt. "I am your mother."

"Then act like a mother!" Jordan's words were sharp, but considering the fiascoes during their last visit, Valene knew it was necessary that some ground rules be established if they were to get through the day without a major confrontation.

"Do we understand one another, Mother?" Jordan asked, tapping his toe impatiently.

"Oh, Jordan, don't be silly." His mother gave them both a warm smile that was about as genuine as a ten-dollar Rolex watch for sale on the streets of Times Square. "It's Christmas. Of course, we're glad you brought your little friend along, and if you feel you have to have that dog with you as well, I guess I'll have to put up with it."

"Good, then we understand each other." Jordan gave Hero a quick pat on the head, then smiled up at his mother. "Why don't you show Valene the Christmas tree while I get some things from my pickup?"

Although she looked none too happy about his request,

Margaret motioned for Valene to follow and led her into the living room. Valene caught her breath as she stood before the perfectly shaped Christmas tree. What looked to be a thousand tiny gold lights wound their way through its branches. And from its tip to nearly the floor, the tree was covered with hundreds of gold-colored ornaments and countless bands of shiny gold garland. It was magnificent, as were all the other decorations in the room.

"It's lovely," Valene said, stepping back for a better look. "I've never seen anything like it."

"I use the same designer every year. He's very much in demand, but I'm at the top of his list."

Valene's eyes widened. "You don't decorate your own tree?" She'd always thought decorating the tree was one of the highlights of the season. She loved decorating her family's tree.

"Of course not! Why would anyone want to decorate their own tree? It's so time-consuming, and I'm sure those branches are quite prickly."

"There you are!"

Valene turned at the sound of Jordan's voice and found him pulling Hero in a little red wagon that was just large enough to hold his body.

"Look at Hero," he said pointing proudly to the dog. "I've been taking him for a ride. This was my old wagon. If we'd gotten him something like this when we brought him home from the vet's, Valene, then I wouldn't have had to sleep in your bed."

Margaret looked as though she was going to faint. "You—you slept in her bed?"

Jordan grinned. "Sure did. For several weeks."

His mother's hand went to her forehead as she let out a sigh of exasperation. "You needn't brag about it. Gentlemen usually keep their conquests to themselves."

He threw his head back with a robust laugh. "Mother, Hero couldn't be moved. And since he was too heavy for Valene to lift when he needed to be helped or cleaned up, we switched condos at night. She stayed in mine. I stayed in hers. It was all perfectly respectable. Apparently you don't know me or Valene, or you wouldn't have jumped to such a conclusion. We both have values."

Both his parents seemed relieved by his explanation, but neither commented on it, and the rest of the morning was spent on simple chitchat.

After an exorbitantly festive Christmas dinner, the four, along with Hero, moved into the solarium to open their gifts. Although the decorations in the living room had been breathtakingly beautiful, Valene found the solarium decorations more to her liking. The tree, though not as tall, looked more traditional and was filled with multicolored lights and ornaments. Most of the ornaments were the collector type, and no doubt quite expensive, but nonetheless, they were intriguing. Any child would have loved that tree.

Fresh greenery, wrapped with garlands of red and green and silver and entwined with tiny twinkling lights, was draped in half circles around the entire glass ceiling of the huge room. It was like a fairyland. Valene felt herself gawking and wondered what Mrs. Young would think of her naiveté. She'd never been around such blatant extravagance.

Once they were all settled and Hero was confined to the throw rug the maid had provided for him, they began to exchange presents. Valene handed Margaret her gift with trepidation—a large family-tree sampler she'd cross-stitched, with the names and birth dates of the past five generations of the Young family. Valene had loved stitching it. Evenings,

Jordan would sit in the chair, watching her, smiling his approval. He'd even insisted that she stitch her name and the date in the lower right-hand corner. When she'd said his mother might not approve of that, he'd insisted, saying she was going to be part of the family, and her name should be there. It'd been a wonderful experience for both of them. They'd taken it to a store and had it matted and mounted in a lovely gold-edged frame.

She held her breath as she watched Margaret examine the package. Valene had been especially careful with the wrapping, using a lovely paper she'd found at a neighborhood store and some gold ribbon she'd been saving for a special occasion.

After reading the card, Margaret sent a mere flash of a look toward Valene, then proceeded to open her gift. Valene nudged Jordan, and he turned to watch.

Margaret pulled off the wrapping, opened the box, pushed aside the tissue paper, and frowned. Then with only an obligatory smile, she said, "How quaint," and put it aside.

Valene's heart sank. She'd spend every free minute since Thanksgiving working on that sampler, and Margaret had barely looked at it.

"Valene made that for you herself, Mother!" Jordan reached over and picked up the frame, holding it up for his mother to see. "It's our family tree!"

"So it is. How nice." Margaret quickly turned her attention to her next gift.

Valene put her hand on Jordan's arm and said in a mere whisper, "It's okay. Let it rest. Don't say anything, please."

Although his face was filled with frustration, he gave her a half smile and leaned back in his chair.

"Oh, Jordan, these are great!" his father said, smiling as he took a pair of golf gloves from their box. "I've been intending to get a new pair. Thank you."

Several presents under the tree were for Valene, all of them from Jordan. She loved each thing he'd selected for her. His parents gave him an abundance of gifts, mostly things she doubted he'd ever use. His tastes were not nearly as grandiose as theirs.

When the last package had been opened, Jordan turned to her, a frown etching its way onto his face. "What did my parents give you, Valene?"

She tried to avoid his eyes, knowing her answer would upset him, and whispered, "It's okay, Jordan. There really isn't anything I need."

His expression quickly turned to one of anger as he rose and pointed a finger at his mother. "You've known for over two weeks I was bringing Valene with me, and you didn't even get her a gift? You give gifts to your hairdresser, your mailman! You even give them to the UPS man! Why not Valene?"

His mother met his angry face with one of her own. "Because I'd hoped you'd come to your senses before Christmas Day and break up with that little fortune hunter, that's why! Can't you see, Jordan? She's way beneath you!"

Jordan closed his eyes and drew in several deep breaths. Valene knew he was struggling to control his temper.

He grabbed her by the arm and pulled her up beside him. "Give me your ring, Valene!"

She reached into the neck of her sweater and caught hold of the fine gold chain Jordan had bought for her to hold her ring until they could tell his parents they were engaged. He'd planned to do a grand presentation when he told them, dropping to one knee, much like he had at her parent's house. He'd wanted his parents to share in their joy. But as Valene had feared, it hadn't happened. Nothing that day had gone like they'd hoped.

She pulled back the lobster-claw clasp, slid the ring from the chain, and handed it to him.

Jordan laid it in his palm and extended his hand. "See!" he said, his voice still tinged with anger. "This is our engagement ring. I've asked Valene to marry me, and she's said yes. She's going to be Mrs. Jordan Young as soon as I can talk her into setting a date!"

His mother gasped and began to fan herself. His father simply stared at them.

"What about the navy? Our plans for your future?" Colin asked, taking their news a bit more calmly than his wife.

"We've worked those things out, Dad."

Margaret stood to her feet, her face nearly as red as her caftan as she glared at her son. "I forbid it, Jordan! I absolutely forbid it! You will not marry that girl!"

Jordan took Valene's left hand in his and slipped the diamond solitaire onto her third finger. "I am going to marry Valene, and there's nothing you can do to stop me. You're a hateful woman, Mother. You're your own worst enemy. I can't see how Father has put up with you all these years."

Colin stepped in between them, his face now reddening. "You have no right to talk to your mother than way, Jordan! Apologize right now."

Jordan shook his head vehemently. "Apologize? For what? All I've said is the truth!"

"I'm so disappointed in you, Jordan," his mother said, moving to stand by her husband. "Don't you realize how important it is for a man of your position to have a wife with a fine background and the necessary social graces? Someday you're going to take over your father's business. The woman who will become Mrs. Jordan Young needs to be—"

"Someone like you? Someone whose rung on the social

ladder is more important than having values?"

"Take it from me, Son, those things do count," his father interjected. "Your mother has won over many a business client with her social graces and her business acumen."

"Well then," Jordan said, his voice still sounding sharp. "I guess maybe the family plans will have to change. Perhaps you'd better find someone else to run the Young corporation, because I'm marrying Valene—whether you like it or not!"

Valene couldn't believe what he was saying. "But—"

Jordan took her arm with one hand and grabbed onto Hero's leash with the other, then strode toward the door. "Get used to it, folks. Valene Zobel is going to become Mrs. Jordan Young, my wife, and there's nothing you can do to stop us."

He rushed through the house and out to his Avalanche, which was still parked in the circular drive, dragging Valene and Hero behind him.

"Jordan, you can't leave like this!" his father bellowed out, panting for breath as he caught up with them.

"You marry that tramp, and you're no son of mine!" His mother looked as if she was about to burst with anger as she hurried toward them.

"What about our things?" Valene asked as Jordan opened the passenger door and nearly shoved her inside.

He carefully lifted Hero and placed him on the backseat. "Forget about them," he answered as he slammed the door and ran around to the driver's side. "We're getting out of here."

Valene took a quick backward glance as they turned onto the road. Standing in the middle of the circular drive, both Mr. and Mrs. Young stood screaming at them. Especially Jordan's mother. Valene's heart ached. Although Jordan seemed willing to give everything up for her, she wasn't sure she could let him do it.

They were about half way back to Spring Valley when his cell phone rang, but he ignored it.

"You'd better answer it. It might the base calling you."

"Or my parents with more advice?"

"Answer it, Jordan. Please."

He pulled the phone from his belt and punched one of the little buttons.

From the serious look on his face after he'd said, "Hello," she knew the call wasn't from the base.

ten

"Dad's had a heart attack," Jordan announced as soon as he finished the call. "The ambulance is on its way."

Jordan waited for a clearing in the traffic, then spun the pickup around and headed back toward La Jolla.

Valene began to sob uncontrollably. "It's all my fault. If you hadn't taken me with you, this would never have happened. Oh, Jordan, what if he doesn't make it?"

"He's got to make it." His fingers tightened on the steering wheel. "I should've known something like this was going to happen. He had a mild heart attack last year. The doctor insisted he slow down some and alter his diet, but other than that, he's been fine."

"We did it to him. If we hadn't upset him with our news, this would never have happened." Valene's guilt was almost too much to bear. "Your poor mother must be terrified."

He gave her a puzzled look. "After all she's done to you, you're still concerned about her? Her rage didn't help my father any. She's as much to blame as we are."

"But she loves your father. She must be frantic! I wish there was something we could do."

He turned toward her quickly. "You want to do something? Then pray, Valene. Ask God to keep my father alive!"

She nodded, grateful for his suggestion. "Lord," she said, bowing her head, "we don't know much about Colin's condition—just that he's had a heart attack. But You know. If it be in Your Will, we ask not only that You would spare his life, but that You would give him many more years. You are the

Giver of Life, the Great Physician. Be with him now. Restore him to health, and I ask You to be with Jordan's mother too. Comfort her, Lord. Give her a sense of peace. I ask all these things in Your name, amen."

"Thanks, Valene." Jordan's softened features and his smile told her he appreciated her prayer.

When they reached the hospital, they were told Colin was alive and led to the cardiac care unit. Margaret, who was crying hysterically, rushed to her son and buried her head in his chest.

Jordan wrapped his arms about her and pulled her close, patting her back much like he would a child who'd been hurt. "He's going to be alright, Mother," he told her confidently. "He's in good hands now. I'm sure they're doing everything they can."

She lifted a mascara-stained face to his. "H—he was so upset when you left, and he accused me of running you off. H—he went into the den and slammed the door behind him. I heard a crash, and when I rushed in to see if he was alright, I found him lying on the floor next to his desk." She burst into tears again, her chest heaving uncontrollably.

Valene wanted to rush to the woman and throw her arms about her, even though she knew that would only upset Margaret even more. Jordan put out a hand and motioned her to come to him. She shook her head, but he motioned again. She crept over silently, hoping his mother wouldn't notice.

Margaret lifted her face from his chest and stared at Valene coldly, without saying a word. Valene could see the woman's attitude toward her had not changed one bit.

"When I heard about Father's heart attack," Jordan said, "I asked Valene to pray for him, and she did. I want her to pray again." Jordan slipped his free arm about Valene and pulled her close.

Valene was humbled by his request. She bowed her head and prayed aloud, a prayer much like she'd prayed earlier. When she finished, she found Margaret's harsh expression had softened, and some of the bitterness she'd displayed earlier that day had vanished.

"You can go in now, but only for a few minutes," a nurse told Mrs. Young. Jordan and Valene stood holding hands, watching until the heavy double doors closed behind her.

It seemed an eternity before Margaret came back, although they knew it had to be no more than five minutes.

"How is he?" Jordan asked quickly.

Margaret blinked hard. "He's so still. I'm worried about him. I—I don't know what I'll do if he doesn't make it."

The three huddled together in the waiting room all night, with Jordan asking Valene to pray several more times, and he and his mother alternating the once-an-hour visits. At dawn, the doctor announced Colin had regained consciousness, and things were looking somewhat better. Although Colin was quite weak, the doctor encouraged them to continue their visits, just not to tire him by letting him try to talk.

Jordan took Valene by the hand and begged her, with pleading eyes, to go in and see his father. "Lay your hands on him, Valene, and pray for him. Please. He needs your prayers."

"But won't it upset him to see me there?" The last thing she wanted to do was get the man agitated by her presence.

"No. When I told him I was going to ask you to come in and pray for him, he blinked at me. I think he wants you there."

"I'm not so sure that's wise," Margaret said, grabbing Jordan's arm. "She's right. It may upset him."

"I know Father wants her there." He gently freed himself

from his mother's hold and led Valene to the double doors. "Go on, Sweetheart, please."

Valene ventured into the little cubicle with apprehension, but when she thought she detected the faintest smile on Mr. Young's face, she knew God would help her. She tiptoed to his bed and touched the helpless man's arm. His face was nearly as white as the sheets. "Hi," she said softly. "Jordan asked me to come in and pray for you."

He blinked. Taking that as a sign he was agreeable, she patted his arm and began to pray, asking God to heal him and restore him to health. When she finished, she was sure his faint smile had broadened. She told him she'd continue to pray for him and excused herself. Praying for the man, like Jordan had asked, had been much easier than she'd imagined.

❧

A couple weeks later, as Valene and Jordan sat beside his father's recliner in the hospital room, Colin begged Jordan to resign from the navy and take over as CEO of Perfection Plastics in his place. With difficulty, he explained the doctor had told him his recovery was going to be slow and hard, and even if he was able to get most of his strength back, he was going to have to rid his life of much of its stress.

Valene, feeling the conversation should be between the two men, excused herself and headed toward the little chapel on the main floor, where she intended to pray that God would lead Jordan to make the right decision, the one God would have him make.

She was about to go into the chapel when one of the hospital custodians, a tall, gaunt-looking man who was cleaning up a spill from the floor, approached her.

"Hey," the man said, sticking his mop back into the bucket. "Ain't you related to that snooty Margaret woman?

The one married to that guy who had the heart attack?"

"Do you mean Margaret Young?" She was surprised by his question.

"Yeah, I guess that's her name. I've been cleanin' her husband's room."

"No, I'm not related, but I am engaged to her son. Do you know her?" The chance of this man knowing Margaret Young seemed quite unlikely, but he had aroused her curiosity.

"Sure do. Her and me used to date when we was in high school in Nevada—long time before she married that guy upstairs. But she wasn't the high and mighty Margaret then. She was Maggie. We was both raised in the poor section of town. She lived in an old, broken-down trailer park, just like me. Her daddy was the town drunk."

He let loose a snicker, his grin lacking two front teeth. "That man spent more time in jail than he did at home. Don't think he worked a day in his life. Even less than my pa did."

Valene shook her head. Was this really happening? Surely the man had made a mistake. The woman he was describing couldn't be Margaret Young. "Didn't she have a mother?"

"She was workin' at the bar down on the corner some of the time. Home gettin' drunk with her hubby the rest of the time, I guess. Never saw much of her, but that Maggie was sumpthin'. Dated nearly every boy in town. She had a terrible reputation, if you know what I mean."

His snide laugh made Valene shudder.

"Yep, she was one tough cookie. Nuthin' but trailer trash. Last time I saw her, she was broke, pregnant, and unmarried, leavin' town in her old wreck of a car. Sure makes you wonder how she snagged that rich old geezer layin' up there in that bed. He seems like a right nice old fella."

Valene stood gaping, stunned by his words. *Broke, pregnant, and unmarried? He has to be talking about another Margaret.* "Are—are you sure you don't have the wrong person? Margaret is a fairly common name."

"It's her alright. I'd know her anywhere, despite them fine clothes and that fancy hair. You ask her! Ask her if her maiden name used to be Clark, and if she was from Dingo, Nevada. Then you'll know I'm tellin' you the truth."

Val stared open-mouthed as the man and his bucket moved on down the corridor. She knew she must keep his story to herself. If it was true, she had no right to tell it. If it wasn't true, telling it would serve no purpose.

By the time she'd prayed and returned to Colin's room, the two men had reached a decision. Jordan would resign from the navy in three months when his obligation was over and take over as CEO at Perfection Plastics. Although Valene felt left out of the decision-making process, she knew they'd made the right decision, considering the state of Colin Young's health.

"I don't know about you, Valene," Jordan said as the two sat quietly in her condo that night, "but I'd like to have a February wedding at Seaside Chapel. Maybe on Valentine's Day. I need you by my side as my wife when I take over Father's position."

"I'd like that too. I know your mother doesn't approve of me, but I'm still hoping, once she realizes she can't stop our plans to get married, she'll give in and accept the idea."

"I don't remember Mother ever giving in on anything. Wait'll she hears we're having our wedding in Granite Cliff. That'll set her off!"

⋙

"Absolutely not!" Margaret said, stomping her foot against the floor when they went to visit Jordan's father the next weekend. "Jordan, you are our only child, and you are going to have a proper society wedding, even though you aren't marrying one of your own kind!"

Valene bit her lip, trying to maintain her silence, deciding to let Jordan handle his mother's objections rather than blunder in and say something she'd later regret.

"I'll pretend I didn't hear that remark. I only hope Valene can forgive you. But you have to be reasonable, Mother! Father has just come through a heart attack. I'm going to have to wrap things up at the navy and take over a position I'm not prepared for, and I want to marry Valene as soon as possible. I need her to help me face the coming days. She's going to be your daughter-in-law. I'd think you'd want to start getting along with her. Even if we wanted it, which we don't, there isn't time to plan the kind of wedding you're talking about."

"Jordan, think! That girl is nothing but a tramp. A nobody. Can't you see she's not good for you?"

"Write February 14 on your calendar, Mother," Jordan told the irate woman as he stormed toward the door, his fists clenched at his side. "If you want to come. Fine. If not, it's your loss. We are going through with this wedding." He turned to Valene. "I'm going for a walk to clear my head. I'll be back in a little while."

"You're the cause of this!" Margaret said, turning her wrath on Valene and shaking her finger in her face. "You're not worthy of the being a Young!"

"Oh? But you are, Maggie Clark?" Valene blurted out before she could stop herself. From the look on Margaret's face, she knew the custodian had been telling her the truth. Maggie Clark and Margaret Young were one and the same person.

Margaret's face turned a sickly yellow as she let out a gasp. Her hands dropped to her sides.

"You are Maggie Clark from Dingo, Nevada, aren't you?" Valene asked, trying not to sound vindictive.

Margaret grabbed the armrest and lowered herself into a chair as she stared at Valene. "Who told you about me?"

Valene sat down opposite the distraught woman, her insides a jumble of nerves. "Th–that's not important."

Margaret's hands trembled. "Ha–have you told Jordan?"

The look on Margaret's face melted some of the hurt Valene had suffered at the woman's hands. "I've told no one."

Margaret fell on her knees at Valene's feet, tears running down her cheeks, a penitent look on her face. "Please, Valene, I beg you! Don't tell anyone. It would ruin me! I'll be disgraced, and so will Colin and Jordan. You wouldn't want to do that to the Young family, would you?"

"Have you forgotten? You were willing to push me aside. You said awful things about me to Jordan. Why should I be concerned about you?" In her heart, Valene knew she'd never betray the woman's secret, but she had to admit it felt good to see Margaret on her knees, contrite.

"I'll make a deal with you," Margaret said, cupping Valene's knees with her well-manicured hands. "Keep my secret, and I'll stop interfering between you and my son."

The woman's words shocked Valene. Make a deal?

"Please! I mean it. I'll do anything you ask, only don't let anyone find out about my past. All these years I've lived with the fear that someone would come along and expose me. I never thought it would be you."

"I–I must know about the baby you were carrying when you left Dingo. Was it Jordan?" The question had preyed on Val's mind since she'd first heard about Margaret's pregnancy.

The woman shook her head sadly. "No, it wasn't Jordan. I–I had an abortion. I've never forgiven myself for that. I nearly lost Jordan when he was born, and I've always thought it was God's way of punishing me for what I'd done." She placed her head in Valene's lap and wept until it seemed she could weep no more. "I'm so, so sorry."

Despite the way Margaret had talked about her, Valene's heart went out to the woman. All these years she'd held onto her precious financial and social standing, knowing her house of cards could come tumbling down any minute. But how could Val possibly keep something like this from Jordan? Something that would influence all of their lives if it ever came out? Wouldn't she be living the same sort of lie as Margaret? Fearing someday he'd find out she'd kept something this important from him, and he'd be furious with her?

But then again, she had no right to tell him. It was his mother's secret, not hers. "I don't know if I can promise something like that. I'll—I'll have to pray about it before I can give you an answer."

For the next few days, Valene agonized in prayer. Finally God gave her the answer she was seeking. One she could never have thought of on her own.

The following weekend, when they went to visit Jordan's father again, Valene faced Margaret confidently.

"Whatever you ask, I'll do," Margaret said with pleading eyes as she held onto Valene's arm. "Just tell me."

"First, I want you to start treating me with respect. No more of this she's-not-your-kind talk. I want to be treated as your equal."

Margaret hesitated. "I'll do it. I promise."

"Second," Valene said as she counted her requests off on her fingers, "you have to accept me as your future daughter-in-law and stop trying to break Jordan and me apart."

"I promise, if you promise not to betray me."

"Third. I want you to be nice to my dog. He's very important to me, and he's important to Jordan."

"Yes, if I have to, I will."

"Fourth. . .this one you may find quite difficult, but I consider it to be of the utmost importance."

"Anything."

"I want you to start attending church at—"

For the first time, Margaret smiled. "Oh, that won't be hard. I always go to church on Christmas and Easter, at that big new church downtown. Many of our friends and business associates attend there. They have such wonderful bazaars."

Valene lifted her hand. "You didn't let me finish. I want you to start attending church every Sunday, and I want to approve of the church you attend. It must be a Bible-believing, Bible-preaching church. Sickness will be your only excuse for not attending."

Margaret's eyes widened. "Every Sunday? And you're going to pick out the church? Isn't that a bit extreme?"

Valene shrugged. "Not if you want me to keep your secret. It's up to you, but I have one more condition."

"I'll pay you whatever you want!" the woman said quickly.

"I don't want money. I want a signed and dated document, written in your own hand, saying that if the truth ever comes out, you'll tell Jordan I only agreed to keeping this secret because I didn't want to hurt him or Colin. Will you do that?"

"Yes, of course, if I have no other choice. But how do I know the person who told you won't talk?"

"You don't, and neither do I, though I doubt he will. He could've said something years ago, and he didn't. I guess it's a chance you'll have to take."

Margaret seemed to think Valene's words over carefully before pulling a piece of paper from the desk and beginning to write. Valene read it through when the older woman finished. Everything she'd asked was included. "I guess this means we've come to an agreement."

Margaret gave her a grateful smile. "Yes, Valene, we have an agreement." To Valene's surprise, the woman threw her arms about her neck and gave her a hug.

"Thank you, Valene. Anyone else would've called the newspapers with my story. You didn't. I now realize you truly love my son and have the best interests of the Young family at heart. I'll never speak badly of you again."

That night, as Valene lay in her bed, she thanked God for showing her how to deal with what she'd learned about Margaret. Through it, He had touched her and made her realize she was as important to Him as anyone. That money and power couldn't buy true happiness. True happiness could only come from a close relationship with Him.

No one was allowed to be married in Seaside Chapel without participating in premarital counseling with Pastor MacIntosh. Although Jordan seemed apprehensive about it when Valene had first told him about the requirement, he agreed, and they attended their first session. After covering the basics, the pastor turned to Jordan and asked, "Do you have a personal relationship with God?"

"As you know," he answered, "I've been attending church here most every Sunday since Valene and I got together, and I've visited with a navy chaplain a number of times. Although I accepted Christ as my Savior when I was ten, I've never felt worthy of His love. I still don't. I find it hard to believe He would forgive me for the things I've done in my life, even though I've confessed them to Him."

Valene stared at him. *What things? He's never told me about anything he's done that would make him feel so unworthy. Do I really know Jordan? From all I've heard from his parents, he was an exemplary child and a perfect son. I've seen dozens of awards he's received from the navy. He's never been in any scrapes with*

the law or caused anyone any trouble that I've ever heard of.
What could he have done that's so terrible?

She watched Jordan's reaction as he and Pastor MacIntosh talked, but she couldn't read any meaning in it.

When she mentioned the issue to Jordan that evening, he broke down and started crying. She sat down beside him and began stroking his back. It pained her to see him so upset. Something was troubling him, but what?

"I have a confession to make," he told her, lifting watery eyes. "One that will shock you and could ruin my family's reputation."

Valene's thoughts instantly went to the secret she was already keeping to avoid ruining the Young family's reputation. Did Jordan know about his mother after all?"

"I've done something, Valene," he said, clenching and unclenching his fists. "Something I'm terribly ashamed of. No one knows but me. That's why I haven't been able to accept God's full forgiveness. I'm afraid if I do, He'll expect me to make my sins public. I wouldn't mind it so much for me, but I have Mother and Father to consider, and now I have you. You may not want to marry me when you hear what I'm about to tell you."

eleven

"Nothing you could tell me would make me love you any less. Whatever it is, we'll face it together." Valene spoke with calm assuredness.

"The weekend before I left for Annapolis," Jordan explained, "some of my friends and I were carousing around in the new red convertible my parents bought for me. We'd each had about six or seven beers, and since I rarely drank, they went right to my head and made me dizzy. Then I got sick to my stomach. I remember letting my friends off at their houses and heading toward home, but I was light-headed and nauseous. From there on, I don't remember anything else about that evening. I don't even remember driving into our driveway and going to bed. But the next morning, when I went out to my car, there was a big dent in the fender, and one of the headlights had been busted out. I didn't have the faintest idea how it'd happened and thought maybe some kids had done it as a prank."

"Maybe they did," she said, hanging on his every word.

"No, that wasn't what happened! When I went back into the house to tell my father about the car, he and my mother were talking about something he'd read in the morning paper. Someone had hit a pedestrian walking along Beacon Road, the same road I always took home. Apparently he'd been hit by a red car, and its driver hadn't even stopped. A patrolman had found the injured man and taken him to the hospital, but he was in serious condition. I'm sure I was the one who'd hit him. I've been afraid to tell anyone. I knew I'd be put in jail for hit-and-run, and I'd never have the navy career I'd planned."

Valene held her breath, willing him to continue.

"I took my car to a body and fender shop in a town about a hundred miles away and had it fixed before anyone noticed, then drove back and finished packing up my things for Annapolis. All these years I've carried the guilt of what I'd done, never able to put it out of my mind. Then when I almost hit Jeff and ended up hitting Hero, it all came rushing back to me. It was déjà vu all over again. That's why I freaked out that day. I knew I could never run away from my responsibilities again. I think I was hoping that paying Hero's bills and helping you take care of him would somewhat absolve me for what I didn't do all those years ago."

"Di–did the man d–die?" she asked, almost fearing to hear the answer.

"No, he didn't die. According to the report on the news, the man was alive but badly hurt. His wounds weren't fatal."

Valene wrapped her arms around him. "Jordan, dearest, dearest Jordan, don't you know there isn't anything God can't forgive? You don't need to carry this burden of guilt. Let Him carry it for you."

"I have to do something, Valene," Jordan said, rising and squaring his shoulders. "I have to make things right with that man. The one I hit with my car. I have to ask his forgiveness and try to make restitution. Regardless of the circumstances."

The next day, they went to the La Jolla newspaper's morgue, looked up the story on the accident, and wrote down the man's name and address.

"I hope he still lives here," Jordan said as he knocked on the door later that day.

The door creaked open, and the man they were looking for invited them in, but as Jordan began his story and told him what a coward he'd been, the man seemed confused.

"It wasn't a red car that hit me; it was a black truck. As usual, the newspapers got their story all wrong. They arrested the guy for drunk driving several months later, and he confessed he'd hit me and left me there. It wasn't you!"

Valene shrieked with joy as Jordan grabbed her up in his arms and danced about the room. The man stared at them, still looking bewildered.

"All these years I've carried the guilt of nearly killing a man and abandoning him, and I didn't even do it! It must've been kids vandalizing my car after all! Praise God, Valene! Praise God! I'm finally free!"

❧

Valene leaped for the telephone when it rang in her old bedroom in her parents' house.

"Hi," a male voice said softly on the other end. "Know what day this is?"

"Umm, Valentine's Day?" she asked dreamily, loving the sound of that voice.

"Yes, it's Valentine's Day. But what else is it?"

"Umm, Saturday?"

"Yes, it's Saturday, but it's also your wedding day, unless you've changed your mind."

She cupped the phone tightly. "I'd never change my mind about marrying you, Jordan Young. You're gonna be stuck with me for life."

"Is that a promise?"

"That's a promise."

"See you at the church."

"Wait," she said, "someone wants to talk to you." She held

the receiver out toward Hero. "Speak!"

The big dog barked loudly.

"He said he loves you too."

Jordan laughed. "Tell him I love him, and don't forget to bring him to the church. I have a boutonniere for him to wear. After all, he's the one who brought us together."

"I love you, Jordan."

"I love you, Valene."

&

"You look beautiful, Sis." Vanessa stared at her twin sister. "That gown is gorgeous. I've never seen anything like it."

Valene tilted her head as she looked in the mirror. "I would never have picked out a wedding gown quite this ostentatious, but it was the one concession my future mother-in-law asked, that she get to provide my wedding dress. I couldn't refuse her offer. I have to admit, I do like it! It makes me feel like a princess. You know, I've almost gotten to like that woman, now that she's come down from her throne!" she added with a laugh.

"I just want you to be happy. Jordan's a wonderful man. You did good, Sis!"

"May I have a few minutes alone with Valene?" Margaret Young asked, pushing the dressing room door open a crack.

"Sure." Vanessa picked up her bouquet and moved into the hall. "I'll be right outside if you need me."

Margaret stared at Valene with misty eyes. "You—you are so beautiful, Dear. The loveliest bride I've ever seen."

Valene wrapped her arm around her future mother-in-law and gave her a hug. "Thank you. I love the dress."

"I'm glad. I wanted you to like it. I—I just wanted to thank you one more time for keeping my secret. Even after I treated you so badly, you've treated me with nothing but love and kindness. Thanks to you, Colin and I have been attending that church you recommended, and I've heard things I've never heard before about the Bible and what it means to be a Christian. Although I'm not ready to be one yet, I am considering it."

Valene's heart leaped for joy. *Thank You, God!*

"Last Sunday, the preacher talked about God's love, His forgiveness, and His kindness. I've thought about his words a great deal this week, and I've come to a decision." Margaret paused, blinking a few times before going on.

"I've asked way too much of you, Valene, expecting you to keep my secret from Jordan and Colin. I can't go on like this anymore, wondering if someone will show up at our door and tell them. As soon as you two get back from your honeymoon, I'm going to tell both my son and my husband. It'd be better coming from me than someone else. I only hope they can forgive me for keeping this from them all these years. Then I think I'll ask for God's forgiveness."

"I love you, Mother Young," Valene said as she kissed Margaret's cheek.

"Yo—you called me Mother! I—I like that."

A gentle knock sounded on the door, and it opened a crack. "Ready, Sis?" Vanessa asked. "The organist is playing your song."

❧

"That's quite an unusual groomsman you have there," Pastor MacIntosh said, smiling at Jordan as they stood at the front of the church, waiting for the double doors to open.

Jordan grinned as he bent and patted the head of the big black dog wearing a white carnation boutonniere on his new, gold-colored collar. "Hero has to be part of the wedding party. He's the one who brought Valene and me together and kept us together until we got this thing worked out. I think Valene'll be pleased when she sees him here."

Nathan, his best man and newest friend, let out a chuckle. "You mean she doesn't know?"

Jordan shook his head. "Nope, I wanted it to be a surprise. Actually, it was Jeff's idea."

Jeff's broad smile nearly covered his freckled face. "Jordan let me pin that flower thing on Hero's neck."

"Just don't drop the ring, Mr. Ring Bearer," Nathan told his son with a proud grin and a shake of his finger.

Jeff gave him a look of exasperation. "Dad, I've done this before. At your wedding!"

"You may have to hold me up," Jordan told his best man as the organist began to play. "I'm more nervous now than I was when I took my first solo flight."

Nathan gave his arm a quick pinch. "No more solo flights for you, Buddy. From now on, you're flying double!"

"Nope, you're wrong about that. I'll be flying triple. Valene, me, and the Lord!"

As the music swelled, all eyes focused on the back of the sanctuary.

Vanessa looked radiant in her long, pink matron-of-honor dress, but Jordan barely noticed. He was waiting for Valene. When she finally appeared, all dressed in white, her face and shoulders covered by a delicate, nearly transparent veil, he thought she looked like an angel. As she seemed to float down the aisle toward him, he smiled to himself, remembering the look on his bride-to-be's face when his mother had said she wanted to provide the wedding gown.

Only Valene, with her sweet, understanding ways, would have allowed such an unconventional request in light of the way his mother had treated her. She was the perfect woman for him. How thankful he was that they'd each saved themselves for one another. She was his bride, the love of his life, and hopefully the woman who would one day bear his children. *Thank You, God.*

⁂

Although the sanctuary of Seaside Chapel was filled with family and friends, Valene's gaze immediately went to Jordan as she held onto her father's arm and they started down the aisle. *It's actually happening! I'm going to be Mrs. Jordan Young. Oh, God, thank You. Only You could have worked out this miracle.*

A slight movement sent her gaze to the floor next to Jordan. Her heart did a flip as she caught sight of the big black dog who was now able to stand on his own. *Hero! Oh, Jordan, how thoughtful!*

When she reached the front, she bent and gave Hero a loving pat. "Good dog." Then she mouthed *thank you* to Jordan.

He mouthed back, *I love you.*

Everything went exactly as it had at the wedding rehearsal. She and Jordan remembered the vows they'd written and memorized, and Jeff didn't drop the ring.

The pastor smiled at the two of them. "Jordan. Valene. Nearly twenty years ago, my wife and I stood where you're standing, right at this very altar, and repeated our vows before our pastor." He gave them a tender smile. "That was before I went off to Bible school and became your pastor. I'll never forget that godly man's final words to us. They've served us well, and I'd like to pass them on to you. I think they're the secret to a happy and fruitful marriage."

Valene felt Jordan's hand tighten around hers as she turned and gazed into his eyes with adoration.

"Love God. Love one another. And at all times, treat each other with kindness."

In unison, although it had not been planned, both she and Jordan said, "We will."

Pastor MacIntosh continued, "By the power vested in me by the State of California, I now pronounce you, husband and wife. Go forth in peace."

As if on cue, Hero barked his approval.

A Letter To Our Readers

Dear Reader:

In order that we might better contribute to your reading enjoyment, we would appreciate your taking a few minutes to respond to the following questions. We welcome your comments and read each form and letter we receive. When completed, please return to the following:

Fiction Editor
Heartsong Presents
PO Box 719
Uhrichsville, Ohio 44683

1. Did you enjoy reading *Love Is Kind* by Joyce Livingston?
   ❏ Very much! I would like to see more books by this author!
   ❏ Moderately. I would have enjoyed it more if

   _____

   _____

   _____

2. Are you a member of **Heartsong Presents**? ❏ Yes ❏ No
   If no, where did you purchase this book? _____

   _____

3. How would you rate, on a scale from 1 (poor) to 5 (superior),
   the cover design? _____

4. On a scale from 1 (poor) to 10 (superior), please rate the
   following elements.

   ____ Heroine   ____ Plot
   ____ Hero   ____ Inspirational theme
   ____ Setting   ____ Secondary characters

5. These characters were special because_____
_____
_____

6. How has this book inspired your life?_____
_____
_____

7. What settings would you like to see covered in future
   Heartsong Presents books? _____
_____
_____

8. What are some inspirational themes you would like to see
   treated in future books? _____
_____
_____

9. Would you be interested in reading other **Heartsong
   Presents** titles? ❑ Yes   ❑ No

10. Please check your age range:
   ❑ Under 18   ❑ 18-24
   ❑ 25-34   ❑ 35-45
   ❑ 46-55   ❑ Over 55

Name_____
Occupation _____
Address _____
City_____ State_____ Zip_____

VANCOUVER

W hat's the best thing about living in a beautiful modern city—being surrounded by buildings, people, and activity? Or just getting away from it all? Meet four women who hold differing views of life in Canada's jeweled city.

Laugh and cry with these resourceful Canadian women and watch how faith and love uphold them on drifting currents of life.

Contemporary, paperback, 480 pages, 5 ³/₁₆" x 8"

❤ ❤ ❤ ❤ ❤ ❤ ❤ ❤ ❤ ❤ ❤ ❤ ❤ ❤ ❤

❤ ❤ ❤ ❤ ❤ ❤ ❤ ❤ ❤ ❤ ❤ ❤ ❤ ❤ ❤

Presents